When our Amulets Fail us

Abigail Fero

Published by Black Shire Publishing
ISBN: 0692384022
ISBN-13: 978-0692384022

CONTENTS

The Locket

When Mirabel went to bed that night, she knew what awaited her in the darkness of the room. The whisper of her nightgown around her ankles sounded like the whisper of her name and she stood as still as she could, at the side of her bed, not wanting to get in. It was as though the dream hovered over her, waiting for her to fall asleep.

Mirabel stood in front of the door, as she always did in the dream. It loomed over her, dark and threatening, the wood glossy, the engravings staring at her. She looked up and up. The stone archway seemed forever away. She had to knock.

Even though she knew it was a dream, she couldn't wrest herself from it. She never could.

Mirabel knocked, her small fist barely making a sound against the wood. Her mother still heard it. She never failed to answer the door. Mirabel's ears picked up every sound of movement on the other side of the door. The thump of her mother's feet hitting the wooden floors, the slow shuffle as she came to the door.

The doorknob in front of her rattled as her mother twisted it from the other side. Mirabel tried to take a step back but her feet wouldn't budge. She watched in horror as the door splintered in front of her, revealing the figure she dreaded. Her mother's black hair hung in straggles down her dressing gown, her eyes black pits of despair.

"So glad you could come," the woman intoned at her, beckoning at Mirabel with a claw-like finger.

Mirabel's feet moved without her consent, carrying her into the room. The door slammed shut behind her, trapping her in the shadowy bedroom she'd never been in before. Light struggled to break through from somewhere but Mirabel couldn't take her eyes off the woman in front of her.

"I needed something of yours," her mother said, leaning down from her great height, her hand reaching out towards the tiny figure that Mirabel cut.

Mirabel tried to lean away, run away, but her feet were glued to the floorboards, her eyes wide as her mother's sinister hand slowly came towards her, the nails looking sharp enough to cut through the frilly dress Mirabel wore.

Her lungs screamed and Mirabel sat up, breaking through the sticky webs of the dream to burst back into full consciousness. Gasping, she clawed at the bed sheets wrapped around her face, taking a large breath of the frigid air as she managed to free herself. Mirabel's pulse thrummed against the thin skin of her neck.

Her bedroom was dark, the night sky outside bleeding black in through the windows. Mirabel sighed, flopping back against the mattress underneath her. It had been at least two years since the last time she'd had that nightmare. There was no question what had summoned it.

Today was the first day that He would arrive. Her uncle had arranged a suitor for her, when she was ten. Mirabel had yet to meet him. She'd refused to even hear his name. Her mother had managed to pull herself together long enough to insist that the meeting wait until she was twelve. Her uncle had acquiesced but it had only put the inevitable off.

Mirabel climbed out of her bed rather than lay awake. The floor was freezing under her feet but she ignored it, walking towards the large, rectangular windows that framed her bed. Pulling back the heavy curtains from the very edge, she peered outside. There was no hint of a sunrise.

The clock that stood next to the door ticked loudly into the silence. She couldn't see the face or the hands to tell the time but she supposed it didn't matter. The hours would pass either way and He would come. She expected Him quite early.

Mirabel stood there until she saw the first stirrings of the sun. It wouldn't be long before Sarah would be at her door, looking to wake her up. No matter that Mirabel was always awake before the woman entered her room, Sarah always appeared at the same time, like clockwork. It was under her uncle's orders, Mirabel knew. She'd stopped telling the woman that it was unnecessary.

The bell rang for seven on her clock just as the door opened. Mirabel turned to greet Sarah. The woman's greying brown hair was as perfectly coiffed as always, her eyes wrinkling at the edges with her smile.

"Good morning, Miss."

"Good morning, Sarah."

"The bath is waiting for you," Sarah said. Mirabel felt something like surprise but brushed it away. It made sense for her to bathe before meeting Him.

Sarah led the way to the bathing room where the tub waited, steaming. She helped Mirabel out of her nightclothes and into the bath before stepping out of the room. The heat from the water curled the escaped pieces of Mirabel's hair. Brushing the tendrils away, Mirabel eased into the warmth.

Her mind was calm, orderly as always. Though her uncle had been watching her carefully for signs of anxiety, Mirabel felt none. She expected to be handed over to a husband, as she'd always known she would. Her mother often spoke to her of marriage and her uncle had also informed her, from a young age, what was expected of her.

After a leisurely wash, Mirabel ducked under the water to wet her hair. Face prickling at the heat, she smiled up at the ceiling. If she had her choice, every day would be a bath day. It offered the most complete warmth, except for the week in the summer where the sun shone with a vengeance.

Through the distortions of the water, Mirabel saw Sarah's face appear. The woman smiled down at her and waited a moment before beckoning. Mirabel broke through the surface and into Sarah's competent hands. Mirabel was still deemed too young to wash her own hair properly.

Mirabel sat as still as she could as Sarah washed the heavy fall of her hair, combing through it with efficient fingers. The suds were rinsed quickly, with a waiting pitcher. Sarah laughed at the bliss on Mirabel's face.

"Summer isn't too far away," Sarah commented, "and maybe you'll get a trip this year."

Mirabel didn't snort. Sarah grinned down at her, tugging playfully at the ends of her hair. Fetching a towel, the servant woman held it open for Mirabel to climb into. Loathe as she was to leave the heat of the bath, Mirabel knew she had to. Clambering over the lip of the tub, she tumbled into Sarah's arms.

The woman rubbed her briskly.

"The new dress today," Mirabel said, catching a glimpse of the striped fabric out of the corner of her eye. She'd had it fitted weeks ago but this was the first time she was seeing it.

"You have to look your best today," Sarah told her. "And try to smile."

"Smile?"

"Yes, smile. Pretend you're in the bath if you must, but smile. Try to remember that you're a happy child." Sarah pulled Mirabel's head back so they could look each other in the eye.

"I don't feel like a child," Mirabel said.

Sarah sighed. "And I suppose today you leave some of that childhood behind. But still, try to smile. It'll make everything easier."

Every adult she knew but her mother told her to smile. She didn't understand the importance of it herself. Sometimes her mother was the best company Mirabel had, though her mother had demands of her own.

Holding her arms up so Sarah could slip the layers of her new outfit over her head, Mirabel stared at herself in the small, round mirror. Her black eyes stared at her from the pale, round face while Sarah bustled around her.

Her hair was tugged and brushed and pulled up into some hairstyle Mirabel had never worn before. It made her look older. The dress was fitted over her underthings, laced tightly at the back to give her the illusion of a womanly figure. Ruffles draped over the backs of her hands, making her fingers look longer.

"Don't you look a sight," Sarah admired as she stood back when she was done. "Do a turn for me." Mirabel turned dutifully in place while the woman scrutinized her. "Just the shoes then," Sarah said with a nod.

The shoes waited in a special box, at the back of Mirabel's wardrobe. Like everything else she was wearing, they were new.

Ordered and made especially for that important day where she would meet the boy she'd spend the rest of her life with.

Sarah knelt down at her feet and helped her into her shoes. They were buttoned up carefully, snug and a little too tight around her bony ankles. Mirabel wriggled in them, hoping to loosen them up. But like all her shoes, they would take time to become comfortable and around that time, they would be discarded as too worn.

"It's almost time," Sarah said as she stood up. "Try to remember to smile."

Mirabel turned up the corners of her mouth. Sarah laughed and shook her head. The woman opened the door for her and then left her alone in the hallway. Sarah's job regarding Mirabel was done.

Mirabel stood in the hallway, gazing at the picture across from her room. It was a family picture, from when her father had still been with them. Her smile looked different then, just like her mother's.

As she stood there, her stomach growled. Mirabel hadn't eaten yet. Breaking her fast had to wait until she was in the company of her beau. He'd traveled far enough to see her, she was told it was only polite.

While Mirabel herself was nothing special as a marriage prospect, especially with the rumors of her mother, her uncle was something else. With a title, lands and wealth as well, becoming part of his family was something to aspire to. He had no wife and no child and Mirabel stood to inherit everything.

She had been told all of this by her uncle. He wanted her forewarned, he'd said, against people looking to use her. They'd had many chats like those, Mirabel perched on the edge of a leather chair, her uncle looking serious and concerned behind his large, wooden desk. Shaking the cobwebs from her head, she turned away from the picture and the memories.

Her new shoes clacked against the wooden floors as she headed towards the main stairs. She knew they were waiting for her so she didn't linger over the gallery of pictures that was the hallway. Today was not the day for that.

The main stairs were white, streaked marble. They made everything in the two-story foyer bright and cold. At the bottom of the curved stairs, she could make Him out. He was quite small.

Smaller than she expected. No one had told her anything about Him once she'd requested to know nothing of her potential husband.

Mirabel paused at the top of the stairs, one hand resting lightly on the smooth bannister. Her uncle cleared his throat at the bottom of the stairs, startling her. She hadn't seen him there. But his signal was obvious enough and she headed downwards, trying to keep her shoes from making too much noise. Despite her best efforts, the sound echoed through the entrance hall until she stopped at the bottom.

"Mirabel, this is John," her uncle said, waving towards the boy who stood in the middle of the entrance hall. He was only a little taller than herself and looked to be maybe two years older, possibly more. But nothing like she'd expected.

The boy bowed, his earnest face smiling up at her. He looked cheerful, and hopeful. Mirabel didn't smile, though she could hear Sarah's voice telling her to.

"Shall we go eat?" her uncle asked into the silence following the awkward introduction.

It wasn't a proper question because as soon as he asked it, he turned, without waiting for a response and led the way. Mirabel hurried to walk right behind him, leaving John to follow at the back. She didn't want to have to look at him or attempt conversation.

Though they rarely dined in the formal dining hall, she knew the way and could tell that's where they were headed. Her uncle intended to impress John, though the boy's guardian didn't appear to be joining them. That was unexpected. Mirabel thought he would have a host of servants with him and at least one member of family.

The morning meal was stilted. Her uncle, though kind, was stiff in the company of others. Mirabel, herself, had nothing to say and John seemed unsure in her presence. The servants came and went, often times providing the only noise. When all the food was gone and there was no point pulling the meal out any further, her uncle abruptly pushed back his chair and rose.

"The servants will show you to your room," he said to John. Then he turned to Mirabel, his eyes raking over her expression, though what he looked for, she could not tell. "Your mother would like to see you."

Visits to her mother were fraught with uncertainty. She never knew who would be waiting in that room, the mother or the madwoman. But it was a duty she knew she must perform, and at times, it was also a pleasure. Mirabel nodded, glad for the reprieve. Without another look at John, she fled the room in as dignified a manner as possible.

Her mother lived at the top of the manor house. She said she liked the views it afforded her, though Mirabel suspected she liked being out of the way, free to do as she pleased. As she climbed the last set of stairs up to her mother's rooms, Mirabel caught sight of the door and suddenly, her dream awakened in her mind, making her footsteps falter.

There was a creak on the other side of the dark, forbidding door. Her mother was waiting. Mirabel's fingers found the locket that hung from her neck in the middle of her chest. Over and over, her fingers rubbed the same whorls on the face of the locket.

Somehow, it gave her courage, as did the thought of John waiting below. Visiting her mother was preferable to finding herself in his company again so soon. He'd had expectations on his face that she didn't know how to handle.

So Mirabel stood before the large door, looking at it. She couldn't quite bring herself to knock, not with that dream fresh in her mind.

"Mirabel."

Her name floated through the thick wood of the door. Her mother sounded sane enough, even a little bit strong. Mirabel reached out and turned the doorknob, in direct defiance of her fears. She never opened the door herself in the dream.

Her mother was sitting up in the bed, her long black hair brushed over her shoulders, flowing down to curl on the bedcovers. She smiled at Mirabel, the expression lighting her pale face. She reached out with a limp hand to beckon her daughter.

Mirabel shut the door behind her and went to her mother, laying her hand in the outstretched one. She could feel her mother tremble with the effort. Her mother's hand was cold and only tightened briefly before falling to the bedcovers.

"How does he look?"

Sinking onto the stool that sat next to her mother's enormous bed, Mirabel didn't let go of the hand in hers. Before she answered, she scrutinized her mother's face. The madness often lurked beneath the surface of calm. Mirabel never knew when it would emerge.

Once she was satisfied that she couldn't see it, she answered her mother's question. "Young."

"Young?"

Mirabel nodded.

"Older than you," her mother said. "And young enough that he will wait, as he is meant to."

"I expected older," Mirabel said. Most women married men much older and she had expected the same for herself.

"We wanted younger, which you would have known, if you'd let us tell you about it."

Mirabel's mother had conflicting views of Mirabel's marriage. At times she seemed frenzied to stop it. Others, it appeared that she thought it was the best idea. No one ever asked Mirabel what she thought of such things. But then, she supposed she didn't have many thoughts on the subject. Everyone else was more than happy to have them for her.

"Though there is always a danger with the young. Feelings, emotions," her mother said, a frown on her face. Her expression folded easily into a frown, the furrows already dug into her face.

Mirabel's mother didn't think much of feelings or emotions. They were unwanted and unnecessary and led to grief. Mirabel had heard those rants many times, both when her mother was sane and when her mother was raving. She advised Mirabel to stifle any emotions she might have.

"But I know you won't do something so silly as to fall in love." A shadow fell across her mother's face.

Those were words seldom mentioned. Her mother had married for love, against her family's wishes, and her story was something of a warning. Mirabel would marry who she was told to marry. There was no room for rebellion in Mirabel's life. And no room for emotion.

"I don't think I will," Mirabel said. She wasn't quite sure what love was. She'd read about it and tried to feel it for her uncle and her mother, but she could never be sure what she was feeling or if it could be called love.

Her mother's eyes focused on her sharply. Then she grinned, a little manically. "No. I don't think you will either."

The limp hand in Mirabel's pulled away to reach out for the locket that hung around Mirabel's neck. Her mother's fingers traced the border of the locket, round and around. It seemed to glow under the touch and Mirabel pulled away. She didn't like anyone else touching her locket.

"You can go now, Mirabel," her mother said, collapsing back against the pillows that propped her up. Her skin looked waxy as though she'd used all of her strength.

It was the burning in her mother's eyes that made Mirabel get up from the stool and retreat to the door. She knew what that look meant. Now was not the time to linger.

So Mirabel bid her mother a good day and backed out of the door. As she pulled the door shut, she heard the wailing start. Sarah told her not to worry about it. Sometimes the memories overwhelmed her mother, though Mirabel thought it happened most often after she visited.

Sarah found her on the stairs, staring at the wall. Mirabel wasn't quite sure what to do, suddenly not free to wander as she wished.

"Your uncle would like to speak to you," Sarah said, one hand on the bannister, one foot on the stairs as though she'd meant to climb them. "Your mother doing well?"

Mirabel nodded.

"I was worried she would overexcite herself with all this change." Mirabel didn't comment. Sarah didn't expect her to and moved out of the way. "He's in his study," she told Mirabel.

He was waiting for her. Sitting behind his desk, his fingers steepled. He waved her in when he saw her at the open doorway. Mirabel's new shoes clopped until she reached the deep red rug that covered most of the floor.

"How are you feeling?"

Mirabel blinked. Sometimes his abruptness took her aback and she stopped a few paces from the front of his desk. She wasn't sure what he wanted her to say.

"I promised your mother we would wait until your seventeenth birthday."

Mirabel nodded. She'd heard that before as well. It would be a five year engagement for whomever her uncle had selected.

"But it would do for you to get to know each other now. He will be spending a few months with us each year, in order that you become accustomed to him."

"What do I have to do?"

"Spend time with him. Accompanied, of course," he said with a nod, his slanted, watery eyes serious underneath his neatly trimmed eyebrows. He seemed to blend into the room, his brown suit almost matching the desk and the wooden paneling behind him. Only his face and hands stood out.

"Every day?"

He didn't answer at first. Just looked at her. Mirabel twitched under the scrutiny. She didn't particularly want to get to know John, nor spend time in his presence every day. Something about him made her nervous.

"Every day would be best. You have the time, do you not?"

Mirabel's governess had left earlier that year. Her uncle had not replaced the woman and Mirabel spent much of her time alone. She'd become accustomed to that and wasn't sure she wanted anything to change.

But there was an expression on his face that made her neck bow. "Of course, Uncle."

"Good. I believe he is waiting in the library for you. Sarah will be there as well."

She knew a dismissal when she heard one. Turning on one sole, she spun and headed for the door. The library was on the other side of the manor house. Mirabel took her time getting there.

Running her hand along the papered back hallway, Mirabel's other hand caressed the locket around her throat. The silver was warm, as it always was. It was comforting and gave her some strength as she approached the library. In truth, she couldn't say what she was afraid of. John didn't seem frightening.

But still, she could feel sweat along the neckline of her new dress. Mirabel tugged at the tight fabric which felt like it was choking her. The doors were open and John was sitting in one of the window seats that looked out over the orchard.

His hair was sandy colored, cropped short against his skull. His face flashed before her eyes. It was still round with baby fat and full of life. She'd expected someone dull, someone serious. Someone like her uncle.

John turned on the cushion as though he'd heard her. His face lit up when he caught sight of her standing just outside the doors. John threw himself to his feet with less dignity than she expected of him.

Bowing again, John didn't move towards her at all. The room between them was vast. Mirabel could barely make out the details of his face or figure, only that the same earnest expression she'd seen earlier was still there.

"Mirabel," he said, breaking the silence. Her name from his mouth sounded like an experiment. As though he wasn't sure how it would sound or what would happen once he said it.

"John," Mirabel replied, uncertain how to proceed.

She saw Sarah, out of the corner of her eye, ensconced in a leather, wing-backed chair, embroidery circle in her lap. Though she was sewing, carefully, Mirabel knew she was listening. She would stay out of the way but she would always be there.

"I've been looking forward to meeting you for some time now," John said, moving a little closer. She could see the sincerity on his face. "Since I was told we were to be betrothed. I wanted to write you letters but..." His brow furrowed at that.

Mirabel knew he would have been told there would be no contact. Her mother wanted her to have a childhood, while her uncle finally agreed that five years would be long enough for them to get to know each other. But looking at her betrothed, Mirabel wasn't sure five years would be long enough.

"You can write them now," Mirabel said. It was a statement of fact but at the look on his face, one would have assumed she'd expressed desire for such letters.

"I will," John said.

She didn't doubt that he would.

"Do you like to play draughts?" John asked. Her uncle kept a handsome board by one of the rear windows. Mirabel had never seen anyone play it before.

"I don't know how."

"I can teach you."

That was how she spent her first day with her intended. It was more enjoyable than she'd expected and she caught on rather quickly to the nuances of the game. John laughed the first time she beat him.

"I underestimated you," he said with a gleam in his eye. "I won't do it again."

John was three years older than her, she learned, though he seemed her age. She learned a lot about him in those months, whether she wanted to or not. He loved to talk. Sometimes a little too much as Mirabel started to notice patterns to her uncle's absences. Many meals, the two of them were left alone, Sarah sitting in the corner of the room.

The two months went quickly past. She became accustomed to John's presence and thought, vaguely, that she might miss it when it was taken from her. But the time passed without any thought to them and Mirabel found herself waving goodbye to John from the front steps of the manor as his carriage sped away.

Her uncle stood behind her, a hand on her shoulder.

"That's the last of him until next year," he said, his voice grave.

Mirabel twisted to look up at him. "You do not like him." She wasn't sure if she meant it as a question or not.

Her uncle frowned down at her, in thought. "I do not dislike him. And I stand by the reasons he was chosen in the first place. But I have sent a list home to his tutor. His education is lacking in certain areas. Areas which need remedying."

"Will I have a tutor?" Mirabel asked. John often spoke of his tutor and his daily lessons. He spent little time with his family, though some with his younger brother, who shared some of the same lessons.

Peering at her from his greater height, her uncle seemed to take it into consideration. "We shall see."

The rest of the year passed as they used to. The only difference were the letters she received and her mother's agitation whenever Mirabel spoke of John. She did not think to curb her tongue at first for he had become a part of her life, as a matter of course. It wasn't a mistake she made often.

After her thirteenth birthday, John came again. He'd grown a little, putting a little more height between them. His face had also lost some of the roundness but his eyes were the same. So was the smile when he climbed down from the carriage and saw her again for the first time that year.

"You haven't changed at all," were his first words.

Mirabel looked down at herself. She was in a new gown and Sarah had tried her hair up in a new fashion. Mirabel had been dubious about it but, as usual, generally indifferent once it was done. She wasn't sure how to take John's greeting.

He laughed at her confusion, holding out his hands so that he might grasp hers.

"You must have much to tell me," he said.

"Uncle wanted to be here to greet you but unfortunately, he was called away on business," Mirabel responded, feeling awkward.

John looked down at her in surprise. "Is everything in order?"

She nodded, though she didn't know anything about the situation. All she knew was that she'd woken yesterday with him gone. Sarah reassured her and Mirabel hadn't thought about it since, until just this moment. Her uncle often had to absent himself to deal with business.

"Then we'll have to occupy ourselves until he returns. Have you been practicing draughts while I've been away?"

It didn't take long for the two of them to fall back into the rhythm of each other. With nothing else to shape her days, except for visits to her mother, Mirabel followed John's lead. He was more than happy to have her company and they rarely spent time apart.

Her uncle returned after three days, looking tired but unconcerned. He greeted John and took the boy into his study. Mirabel waited in the library, a book in her lap. It took the better part of the afternoon and when John emerged, his face was set in serious lines she didn't often see.

Mirabel didn't comment when he joined her or when he didn't speak for a length of time. If it had anything to do with her, Mirabel knew she'd be told in due course. After a while, John recovered and became himself again.

After that first year of their betrothal, the others followed suit. The only changes were John's stature and growing affection for her. Mirabel saw it in his eyes whenever he looked at her and she thought maybe she understood what love was. At least, she thought she knew what it looked like.

The last year of her engagement came. She'd turned sixteen and was waiting for John to arrive. Dressed in her new clothes, she stood in the entrance hall, knowing how happy it made John to find her waiting for him. Her uncle came to join her after a few hours.

"This is the last year," he told her. "Next year, you will be married."

Mirabel nodded. If she'd ever had reservations, they were distant memories now. John's company was nothing new or strange and while she knew there would be changes once they'd been married, she wasn't afraid.

"He's grown into a fine young man," her uncle said as though the words were difficult to say.

She looked up at him then. "A fit heir?"

"It is your children who will inherit. I have no plans to die anytime soon," he said with a twitch of his lips.

She nodded and looked away from him.

He cleared his throat. It seemed he wanted to say something but couldn't quite find the words. Mirabel waited. He would come to them eventually, as he always did.

"Are you happy with him?"

The question made her start. Mirabel frowned and tossed the words around in her mind. She wasn't sure how to respond. But the growing silence and her uncle's growing concern forced an answer from her.

"I am content."

"I suppose that will do."

And then John arrived, ending the conversation. Her uncle never broached the subject after that, though he spent more time with John during his visit.

John was different as well. The time he spent with her he was gentler and more tender. Under Sarah's watchful eye, they took more walked in the gardens and even beyond them. He spoke long about their coming life together.

"Are you happy?" he asked on one of these walks.

After having been asked that by her uncle, Mirabel already had an answer ready for John. She smiled a little, pleased to be able to respond without hesitation. "I am content."

But he was not satisfied with that answer and stopped her with a hand on her arm. Frowning, he asked, "Merely content?"

"Is that not enough?"

He shook his head. "Not for me."

"I'm not sure I know what happiness is. But I can say I am content without any qualms."

His familiar brow furrowed at that, his wide eyes narrowing as he gazed down at her from his greater height. His eyes searched her face but Mirabel didn't know what he was looking for.

"I am more than content with you, Mirabel," he told her, his voice soft. "Can you not say the same?"

She knew what he wanted her to say but she couldn't. "Contentment is more than most," she said instead, breaking away from his grasp.

"I would choose you above all others," John persisted, following her.

"I have never thought of choice."

John's face crumbled at that statement and he reached out to stop her again. "Do you feel nothing for me? After all our time together?"

Mirabel paused, unsure why he was so upset. "I do feel for you," she said slowly, not sure if she was speaking the truth.

"I would have you love me," he told her, the same earnest look on his face as she'd seen four years before.

Mirabel looked up at him and considered his strong, kind face. She reached out to cup his chin and he grasped her hand eagerly. Pressing a soft kiss to her palm, his eyes beseeched her.

"How can you know what love is?" she asked. No one had thought it worth explaining to her and all her reading did not reveal a satisfactory answer. "I am not certain I know how love feels," she admitted.

Again, his face fell. But only for a moment. "You have a lifetime to learn and I will teach by example."

After that conversation, he didn't stay much longer. He was due to stay three months but he left a few days after their walk. He told her there was much to prepare for their life together but he seemed distant from her.

It was almost five months after that, that Mirabel's mother became ill. The plans for the wedding were put on hold and Mirabel spent much of her time in her mother's room. The smell of the doctor's concoctions made her feel dizzy but she clung to her mother's clammy hand all the same.

Her mother was too weak to be a threat to anyone, so no one objected to Mirabel's continued presence, even during the worst of the rants. Mirabel kept a cold, wet cloth on hand to wipe the perpetual sweat from her mother's white face. She sung lullabies when she thought they would help and the sound of her voice sometimes seemed to soothe her mother. Other times, it threw her into a frenzy.

"He isn't dead," her mother would moan, over and over. "Not dead. Should have killed him!"

Mirabel hated those times. She would shush her mother, trying to keep her from thrashing. Lucid moments were rare but even the restless sleep was better than the ranting.

Some nights, Mirabel fell asleep at her mother's bedside, too tired to walk down the stairs to her own bed. She would wake, still clutching her mother's hand. Or her mother's movements and murmurs would wake her.

One night, it was different. She felt a hand, clamp down on her shoulder and shake her with purpose. Mirabel was tired, groggy from the lack of sleep and the stuffiness in her mother's room. She struggled to wake herself. It was only the persistent shaking and calling of her name that roused her.

"Mother," Mirabel said, seeing who the hand and voice belonged to. "Why are you awake? Do you need something?"

"I need to speak with you," her mother said, her voice deep and strong. A gas lamp burned on her bedside table, stretching shadows across her mother's face.

"What is it?" Mirabel asked, sitting up and brushing her hair away from her face.

"I won't see you married," her mother started, her eyes alight with some inner fire. Mirabel couldn't tell if it was the sanest her mother had looked or the maddest.

Mirabel opened her mouth to protest but her mother shook her head, cutting her off with an impatient sound.

"No, don't argue. I won't. But I need to tell you that I've kept you safe. Safe as I never was."

Mirabel frowned, not understanding. But her mother plowed on, regardless of her confusion.

"Your father is not dead," she said. "I know you were told otherwise. I'm not a widow, I am dishonored."

Mirabel nodded. "Uncle told me." He'd told her when he thought she was old enough to understand some of what he had to tell her. "He left us," Mirabel said, to prove she knew.

Her mother startled at that but recovered quickly. "I loved him," she said, grasping at Mirabel's hand, squeezing it tightly. "And it was my ruin. That is love. Grief and madness and ruin. But I've kept you safe," her mother said again, holding tighter to Mirabel's hands, almost crushing the bones together.

"What have you kept me safe from?" Mirabel asked, still confused and not sure she was fully awake.

"I kept you safe," her mother repeated, leaning towards her, her breath hot on Mirabel's cheek. Too hot.

Reaching up with her free hand, Mirabel brushed the back of her hand against her mother's forehead. She was burning up and the woman grabbed her hand, holding it gratefully against the hot skin.

"Let me get you a wet cloth," Mirabel said, freeing her hands to reach for the bowl next to the bed.

"I have to tell you," her mother said, clutching after her, grabbing hold of her dress and pulling her back to the bed. "I've kept you safe, Mirabel. You won't have to endure what I've endured." She tapped a finger on Mirabel's chest where her heart was. "Whatever else I've done, I've kept you safe," she whispered one more time before she fell back on the bed.

Her breathing increased, before becoming labored and raspy. Frightened, Mirabel ran for the doorway and shouted. Her mother's maid servant emerged from the stairway, her face lit by a candle. The doctor was not far behind.

Mirabel was pushed out of the way as they rushed to help her mother. In the corner of the room, Mirabel watched her mother die. Her uncle came only a few minutes later, once the doctor had declared her dead.

He looked his sister over, his long face made longer by the flickering lamps. Mirabel couldn't look at her mother's still face so she stared at her uncle's unmoving one. His expression was unreadable as he stared down at her, his eyes shadowed.

"Come away, Mirabel," he said after a moment.

He reached out an arm and Mirabel moved just enough to tuck herself underneath. His arm fell over her like a weighted blanket and he ushered her from the room. He escorted her down to her room, where Sarah waited, tears on her face.

Her uncle kissed her forehead and left her with her waiting woman. Mirabel fell into Sarah's waiting arms, her body numb. Even her thoughts refused to move. Sarah patted her and crooned into her hair, rocking her back and forth, but Mirabel didn't cry. She couldn't.

After a bit, Sarah tucked her into her bed, face washed and dressed in her nightclothes. She kept a light burning and placed a cup of hot tea on the table beside the bed. Mirabel watched Sarah leave and fell asleep at once.

The next week passed in a daze. She started receiving letters from John at the end of the week. He entreated her to respond but she couldn't bring herself to. True numbness had settled over her and she couldn't feel anything. Her uncle watched her constantly but they did not talk. He had much to organize.

John appeared at the end of the second week, unexpectedly. He found her in the library, staring at the draughts board. She had barely heard his bootsteps on the floorboards before he'd swept her up in a hard embrace.

Over his shoulder, Mirabel caught sight of Sarah watching them. John's hand stroked her hair, brushing it repetitively down her back. He murmured condolences into her ear, so softly she didn't hear the words.

After a while, he drew back to cup her face. His eyes searched hers.

"How are you?" he asked, a line forming between his eyebrows.

Mirabel looked up at him, feeling nothing. "I am well, John."

Her response brought a greater scrutiny and he tilted her head towards the light so that he could see more clearly. The frown deepened on his face but his touch lightened.

"You have not written back to me," he said.

"I did not know what to say."

At that, he crushed her to him once more, cradling her and rocking her as Sarah had done the night her mother died. Mirabel hung in his grasp and let him try to comfort her. But her feelings did not change and he summoned no emotions in her.

"We can put the wedding off," he told her.

She shook her head. "There is no reason to put the wedding off."

He stared at her, still searching for something. She couldn't say whether or not he found it, but he nodded all the same.

"Don't worry about any of the arrangements," he said.

"I won't."

They were married shortly after her seventeenth birthday. The wedding was as small as they could make it, so soon after a funeral. After the ceremony, John and Mirabel visited her mother's grave where Mirabel laid her wedding bouquet.

"I'm sorry she missed it," John said, his arm encircling Mirabel's waist.

Mirabel didn't say anything, just looked down at the inscription. They only stood there a few minutes before they had to return to the reception. But before the door that would take them back into the chaos, John stopped her with a hand on her arm.

She turned to face him, wondering if he would offer her more platitudes. But there was an uncomfortable look on his face, and underneath that, something hopeful.

"I brought you a wedding present," John said after a moment. "I didn't know when to give it to you."

He reached into his wedding jacket while Mirabel looked on with interest. She hadn't expected a wedding present from him but accepted the brown leather box when he held it out to her. Her hands caressed the smooth leather before she snapped open the lid.

Inside, lay a pearl necklace. Each pearl gleamed dully in the evening light, smooth and round. She could hear John hold his breath while she touched each pearl individually.

"It's beautiful," she told him.

He released his breath with a laugh. "Let me put it on you."

Mirabel turned so that he could slip it over her head and do the clasp up for her. She cradled her locket while he fiddled with the necklace, trying to make it stay on. When he was done, he fingered the pearls and asked to see it.

She swung back around so that he could see how it looked. His face was lit with the same joy that had been on his face most of the day. But then he frowned.

"Why don't we take that old locket off," he said as he reached for it.

Mirabel gasped and flinched away, her hand snapping up to encircle the locket. She cradled the warm metal in her palm, staring at her new husband with wide eyes. He looked back at her, eyes also wide in surprise.

"Just for the reception," he said after a moment of this staring.

She shook her head with vehemence. "No. I never take it off."

"It looks silly, hanging under those pearls," he said almost sharply. It was the first time she'd heard him use that tone with her and she took a step back. His eyes softened immediately. "Mirabel…"

She shook her head, feeling her wedding coif start to tumble. "No. I never take it off." Even the thought of removing the locket made her wince and she tightened her grip on it as though it was in danger of being ripped off.

She couldn't say where the instant panic had come from, only that she had felt it before, when Sarah tried to take it off in order to bathe her as a small child. But she knew she couldn't remove it. Mirabel didn't know how to explain that to John.

"My mother gave it to me," she said.

John's eyes softened further and he apologized, drawing her into an embrace. Resting his head on top of hers, he apologized a second time.

"You can wear them both," he murmured.

They returned to the reception. It went on longer than Mirabel cared for it to and she was exhausted when they were finally able to retire to their new rooms in the manor. She'd only been in them once, when she'd been told of the move.

Her uncle had given them the heir's wing and Mirabel looked around their new rooms with interest. Some of her childhood had followed her into that room and she had a feeling that was due to Sarah. John collapsed in a chair by the window, his head hanging back so that she could only see the long line of his throat and the edge of his chin.

It was strange being alone together. Mirabel couldn't think of any other time they'd been left without a watchful eye. She wondered if she should have felt apprehensive. Certainly it seemed expected and John, always so consistent, even seemed daunted.

But after the first few days of being married, they seemed to fall into a routine. They somehow spent both more and less time together. Her uncle took over John's education, preparing him to inherit the title, the property and all that went with it. Mirabel sometimes found herself at a loss, unsure of where she was supposed to go or what she was to do.

Without her mother to visit or John to keep her busy, she found herself wandering in the gardens more and more. Even in the bad weather, she would go for a walk around and around the paths. Sometimes she ventured into the orchards, when they were quiet. John commented on it once or twice but she would only stare at him and say that she enjoyed it. That was always enough to placate him.

Since the wedding, Mirabel wore the pearls. She didn't take them off at all and they floated above the locket, high on her collarbones. John loved to see her wearing them, though she often caught him staring at the locket.

Lying in bed together, he rested on her chest, fiddling with the pearls. Her eyes were closed, her breathing careful with added weight on her lungs. His hair tickled her neck but it was peaceful, lying there.

"Can I open your locket?" John asked, his fingers questing down to where the locket curled on the end of its chain, under her breastbone.

"No," Mirabel said, snatching it away before he touched it.

He propped himself up, leaning over her. She could feel his shadow but she didn't open her eyes or let go of the locket.

"Why not?" There was surprise in his voice. It was the second time she'd denied him something.

"It doesn't open," she told him.

"I thought you said it was a locket."

"It is, but it doesn't open."

She opened her eyes to find a confused scowl on his face. He wanted to inspect it but she wouldn't let him touch it.

"I'm not going to hurt it," he told her, holding out his hand as though he expected her to just give him the locket.

But she shook her head and refused to be budged. It was only one of two subjects she would not bow to him on.

"Are you happy?" he would ask her from time to time.

And every time he asked, Mirabel would give him the same answer. "I am content."

Sometimes he persisted when he received that answer, as though it was not good enough. Other times, he would merely turn away, perplexed, a worry line between his brows. He knew enough not to ask her if she loved him. Once, he confessed to her he didn't think he could survive hearing her say otherwise. So he didn't ask the question he couldn't bear to have her answer.

After three years, Mirabel got pregnant. Her uncle's delight rivaled John's and Mirabel was pampered to distraction. She now had to be accompanied on her walks through the gardens, though she demanded to be given at least ten paces.

Mirabel couldn't say what she felt at the thought of having a child. She knew she should be pleased but the numbness that had come over her at her mother's death clung tight to whatever emotions she thought she should have. So she let John's joy be enough for the two of them and she smiled when he first felt the baby move in her womb.

The birth was difficult. The doctor assured her that all was well and that it was normal, but Mirabel felt as though she'd been ripped inside out, left with a changeling as her reward. The baby squirmed on her chest, wrapped unhappily in a soft blanket John had chosen.

Though the blanket was pale blue, the baby was a girl. John didn't seem to notice in the early hours of the morning as he tiptoed into the room that was still stifling with the heat of labor. Mirabel lay sweating, dazed and trying to keep the baby from rolling away from her.

When John plucked the baby from her weak arms, Mirabel moaned and thrashed. All she saw was a shadow hovering over her, taking her child. John hushed her.

"It's only me, Mirabel. Look what you've done." There was awe and admiration in his voice as he looked down at their daughter's screwed-up face. The baby cried, waving her free arm wildly in protest.

At his voice, overlaid by her daughter's cries, Mirabel roused. Dragging herself higher up on the pile of pillows behind her, she peeled her eyelids back so that she could watch the two of them. John's face was rapt as he stared at his daughter, one giant finger stroking a red cheek.

"She's beautiful," he said when he felt Mirabel's attention on him.

Mirabel looked at the baby's face, scrutinizing it. She'd read about maternal love and the feeling that she should have somewhere under her breastbone. It wasn't there. She frowned and tried harder as she gazed at her daughter. Still nothing.

The scene John and her daughter made should have stirred something in her heart. Mirabel knew that much and there was a flutter of panic that it didn't. John didn't seem to notice, absorbed by the baby.

"What shall we call her?" John whispered after a moment, when their daughter had quieted, hiccupping.

Mirabel didn't have an answer. She looked at the baby and frowned. No name came to mind. It hadn't occurred to her that she would be asked such a question. John and her uncle had seemed convinced she would have a boy and it would be given a family name over which she had no control.

"Name her as you wish," Mirabel finally said, laying herself back down heavily against the pillows. She closed her eyes, ready for sleep.

"No. You can name her. She will wait until you have chosen a name."

And then John laid their baby on her stomach. Leaning over them, he kissed them both on the forehead and left them.

Over the next few days, Mirabel did little but sleep and hold her baby. Once the doctor pronounced the two of them healthy, Sarah took over his duties, looking after them. She also taught Mirabel how to care for her baby. And she reassured Mirabel that her lack of emotions were normal.

"Many mothers feel it," Sarah told her, sitting in a hard, wooden chair, the baby in her arms. Sarah sometimes found it difficult to look away, even when she was talking to Mirabel. "It will pass and you will love her as you are meant to. Don't fret about it, my dear."

Her words did comfort Mirabel. Sarah knew something of children and if she said this was normal, it was. To make up for her lack of love, Mirabel took meticulous care of the baby. She learned how to do everything herself and refused a wet nurse or a governess. This was her child and she would have care of her.

John visited every day, sometimes for hours. He would sit in the same hard chair that Sarah used and hold his baby. Often he was just sit there and say nothing, just stare, a smile scrawled across his face. But he never neglected Mirabel, who he treated with even more tender care than before.

His first words, every day were, "Does she have a name today?"

Mirabel always answered no. But after that first question, he wouldn't press the issue, though Mirabel knew it bothered him. She just couldn't decide on a name.

Sarah brought her books from the library, piled high on the surfaces of the maternity room. Mirabel would flick through them hopelessly and see nothing. Her genealogy was also laid out on the desk so that she could choose a family name if she wished. But still, she saw nothing that leapt out at her. So her daughter carried on being 'the baby' for the first two weeks of her life.

It wasn't until the end of that second week that John noticed her lack of affection. He'd been so wrapped up in his own emotions that he had missed seeing that she had none. He questioned her about it, carefully, as though he wasn't sure what to say or exactly what was wrong.

Mirabel answered as carefully. She was a little ashamed of her lack of feelings for the first time. She could see in John's eyes how distressing he found it and while she felt no love for him either, she didn't want to see him hurt. Especially not by her. He'd been good to her, there was no denying that, and her uncle could have chosen much worse than John.

After that visit, which only lasted a few minutes, his thoughts obviously consuming him, Mirabel decided she had to know. Sarah was happy to watch the baby while Mirabel dressed properly and went for a walk around the manor. She told the serving woman that she felt restless, but Mirabel had a purpose.

She hadn't been up to her mother's rooms since she'd died. She did know that her uncle had ordered them cleaned and tidied but not touched beyond that. Mirabel was grateful and wondered if he'd known she would need to visit them someday.

The door looked smaller as she stood before it. The glossy wood picked up the light from the hall but it wasn't terrifying as it had been before. She felt a compulsion to knock but restrained herself, instead opening the door without permission from anyone but herself.

Even the room looked smaller. The heavy curtains covered the windows, only letting a few lines of light in. Mirabel strode across the room, shaking off the cobwebs of memory. She hauled open the drapes, letting light into the room.

The bed was made, the pillows plumped. The air was chilly in the room and though the fire was laid as though it only waited to be lit, Mirabel knew it hadn't been since her mother died and wouldn't be used again. Nothing in the room would be touched except to be kept clean.

It was strange to see the suit without her mother in it. The life force of the rooms was gone and the rooms almost felt normal. But there was a lurking shadow that made Mirabel shiver.

Telling herself it was just a draught, Mirabel headed for the desk which had been her destination the whole time. She stood in front of it, a little afraid to open it. Most women had dainty writing desks, but not her mother. She had demanded a proper desk.

The surface was uncluttered, cleared away, but the chest that sat on top of it was locked. So were the drawers. And Mirabel was looking for something that would be locked away. Her fingers went to the locket that hung around her neck.

She was afraid to touch anything on the desk though she knew where the keys hung. Her mother had told her that in confidence, during one of her mad moments. They'd never spoken of it again. Her mother's desk had always been something she'd been warned away from.

"I don't want you touching it," her mother had told her more than once. "I'm afraid to let you near it. I don't want you living the mistakes of my life. I did what I had to do so that you won't have to."

When pressed for understanding, her mother's mouth would close up. If pushed any further than a few gentle questions, Mirabel could trigger an episode. So while she knew whatever she needed would be in the desk, she was afraid to look.

But, at the same time, she had to. The keys hung on a little peg, deep in her mother's wardrobe, hidden by clothes left behind. They tinkled in her hand as she hurried towards the desk, eager to get this all over with.

She was looking for a journal, a diary, anything that might tell her of her mother's own experiences. Or something that might illuminate any of her mother's ramblings. Mirabel had high hopes that such a something might exist in the locked drawers and chests of her mother's desk. She couldn't say why she thought the answer might be there.

It was a veritable treasure trove. Mirabel pulled out every book she could find, even the ones that looked like they'd come from the library. When they were stacked on the surface of the desk, Mirabel settled into the chair, hoping to find the answer to her husband's questions.

Mirabel did find the answer. It was scrawled across several of the books and detailed heavily in the journals with some of the same language her mother had often used on her. Mirabel's white face turned whiter, the same shade as her knuckles. Horrified, she couldn't look away, couldn't stop reading, couldn't stop opening book after book and finding the same answer everywhere she looked.

It wasn't until the light had gone from the room entirely that Mirabel found herself able to wrench herself away from the desk. Throwing the books back into the drawers and chests, Mirabel locked them away. She hurled the keys into the dark recesses of the rooms, hearing them clink and skitter across the floor.

Hurrying out of the room, feeling as though she'd saved herself from something sinister, she slammed the door behind her. She ran back to her room, two floors below, startling Sarah as she sat with the baby.

"Everything alright, my dear?" Sarah asked, looking up at her.

Mirabel nodded, flushed and panting. Her hair was strewn about her shoulders and she was sure she must look half mad. She made an effort to pull herself together, tucking her hair back up into the bun, pulling her clothes back into place.

"Just went for a walk," Mirabel said, holding out her arms for her daughter.

Though Sarah looked uncertainly at her, she was happy to place the baby in Mirabel's arms and excuse herself. Mirabel didn't even see her leave. She sat in the vacated chair, her attention fully on her daughter.

"I will keep you safe from me," she told the small, sleeping bundle.

The next day, when John came to visit, Mirabel announced that she had chosen a name. He grinned, the accusations of the previous day forgotten.

"Have you named her after your mother?"

Horrified, Mirabel shook her head. "I've named her after yours."

Delighted, John grinned. And finally, the baby had a name. Mirabel wanted her to have no connection to Mirabel's side of the family and after that, employed both a wet nurse and a governess to take care of the baby. She would stay true to her word and keep her daughter safe.

Mirabel was careful never to let her husband see how little time she spent with their daughter. After her birth, John threw himself into learning the estate that he would inherit. He now had someone to preserve it and grow it for.

Mirabel didn't mind. She was happy to spend the time alone. Her walks grew longer and her thoughts more somber. Eventually servants stopped following her on her rounds of the garden. Mirabel hardly noticed. All she could think of was what she'd read in her mother's books.

It haunted her and even in John's preoccupation, he still noticed, for she was his first love, before the estate and before their daughter. He would comment and check to make sure she was eating.

And while her nightmares grew stronger, John refused to move into a separate room. One night, after a particularly bad nightmare, Mirabel, soaked in sweat, her blood thrumming through her veins, John pulled her close to him. She could feel his heart beating in his chest.

"Mirabel, you must take the locket off. It does you no good."

She frowned and turned in his arms so that the moonlight might show her his face. His eyes were soft until they turned on the locket which lay between them. He reached out for it but Mirabel slapped his hand away.

"You talk about it in your sleep."

Mirabel clutched at the locket, more afraid now than ever. "I need it," she told him.

"I know your mother gave it to you, but I don't think you must wear it every day. It's haunting you."

Her eyes widened.

"At least let us open it," he said. "Maybe that will help."

Her grip tightened and she shook her head. "No. John, we must never open it. It doesn't open," she said, trying to dispel that thought from his head.

He frowned at that. "I'm sure it does."

"No. It does not open. It can never be opened and I can't take it off."

He gazed at her, the softness seeping away. His expression hardened and he grabbed her hand that held the locket.

"Mirabel, this obsession isn't good for you. It isn't good for our daughter. It takes you from us."

She shook her head again, feeling something like tears at the back of her eyes. "It keeps you safe," she said.

"I don't see how it could. It hurts you. I know it does. And the nightmares only get worse. I've held my tongue 'til now but I want the locket gone."

Mirabel cried out at that, feeling something lurch inside her. Fear threatened to overwhelm her. "No, John. Promise me you won't touch it. I can't have you touch it."

"Sarah told me you were in your mother's rooms."

Mirabel nodded. "I had to see it again." She was afraid to tell him that she'd been looking for answers, answers that he had wanted.

"Maybe that has awakened something," he said slowly.

Mirabel nodded frantically at that. "Yes. That. It is not the locket, after all, John. I shouldn't have gone up there but I felt I must. I won't go back."

"Good."

And that seemed to settle it for a while. Their lives settled into a routine as they all became accustomed to their new roles. Mirabel made more of an effort to see her daughter and to spend time together as a family. And it satisfied John for a while, though Mirabel thought she could see him looking at her differently.

Her uncle died when Mirabel's daughter was three. It hadn't been entirely unexpected. He'd slowed down once it seemed that John had a grasp on his responsibilities and duties. He'd died in his sleep, at night.

The funeral wasn't as difficult as her mother's but Mirabel felt strange. There was no one watching over her. All the adults in her life were gone, save Sarah.

John flung himself into the title with vigor and was often away for weeks at a time. Mirabel wasn't sure she missed him, though the house seemed a bit brighter whenever he was home. Their daughter, however, fiercely missed her father when he was away. It was remarked upon by all the servants.

Mirabel's maternal guilt drove her to her daughter when John was away. Though she knew she was no substitute in her daughter's eyes, Mirabel consoled herself that she was trying to be a good mother. The two of them spent most of their time together in the library.

There was a large window in the library that looked out onto the front gates of the manor. Though sometimes John sent word of his return, often he did not and the best place to catch a glimpse of him was from the library. Mirabel would pace with her daughter in her arms, looking out that window.

The pacing only lasted for an hour or so at a time. Once in a while, they would retire to one of the divans that she'd had placed in the library. Reclining on the plush cushions, Mirabel would prop her daughter up on her chest and, stroking her back, the two of them would fall asleep, waiting for John to return.

Mirabel would usually wake before her daughter did. Those soft, still moments when her child slept were peaceful and Mirabel could almost feel the stirrings of something she might call love. But the emotions never blossomed and inevitably, her daughter would wake and Mirabel would be jerked back into reality.

On this one occasion, Mirabel was still sleeping when her child woke. She could feel her daughter move from sleep into wakefulness but Mirabel couldn't pull herself back up from slumber. She drowsed contentedly until her daughter started yanking on the chain that hung around Mirabel's neck.

It wasn't until her daughter actually grabbed the locket, that Mirabel swung into full wakefulness. She yanked the locket from her child's grip, almost upending the girl in her haste to get the locket away from her.

Her daughter looked up at her in shock before breaking into gulping sobs. Tears streamed down her face and Mirabel sat there, staring at her child, the remnants of fear hammering through her veins. A sound behind her interrupted that fear.

It was John, striding through the library, his expression thunderous, his boots loud on the carpeted floors.

"What are you doing?" he demanded, grabbing their daughter from Mirabel's lap.

"She had my locket," Mirabel told him, surprised both to see him and at the look on his face. He'd never looked at her like that before.

"She had your locket?" he repeated.

Mirabel nodded, cradling the locket with as much care as he cradled their child. Mirabel stared up at him in confusion. She'd told him again and again how important the locket was. No one was allowed to touch it but her.

"Mirabel, this is your daughter. She should be more important than that blasted locket." He glared down at her for a moment before marching out of the library, his daughter still cradled carefully in his arms.

Mirabel watched him go, perturbed. The locket was hot in her hand and eventually, she let it fall to her breastbone. She didn't see John again until that night.

He was waiting for her in their bedroom, his arms crossed over his chest. Mirabel smiled faintly at him, wondering if the episode from earlier in the day had passed. John did not smile back.

"That was unacceptable behavior," John said once she shut the door behind her.

"I don't know what you're talking about," she replied, starting the long process of undressing. The row of buttons down her front took patience and concentration.

"It took me an hour to get her to stop crying," John told her.

"She's a baby, she cries."

"You made her cry," John said, his eyebrows in narrow lines over his eyes.

"She needs to learn what she is allowed to touch and what she is not allowed to touch. She needs boundaries and discipline." Mirabel didn't look up from her buttons, working them through the little buttonholes one at a time.

"I want that locket gone."

Mirabel shook her head. They'd had this conversation too many times already and she was weary of it.

"You will not sleep here until it's gone," John said, his voice firm.

His ultimatum surprised her, but not for long. Mirabel wordlessly passed by him, took her nightclothes and followed the hallway to her childhood room. It had been years since she'd been in it last though Sarah made sure it was always kept tidy and free from dust. There were clean sheets on the bed and once Mirabel was dressed appropriately, she climbed in, surprised by how small the bed seemed.

Sleep came easily, her locket in her hand. She barely paused to wonder how John would react.

She didn't see him the next morning when she woke. Mirabel had to fetch clothes from their marital rooms. He wasn't in the dining room either. Mirabel decided not to look too hard for him. When he was ready, he would come find her.

In order to distract herself, and because there was a niggle of guilt, Mirabel went to find her daughter before she went on her daily walk. She heard her before she saw her. The room to her door was open and Mirabel could hear the baby's laughter.

But before she even made it to the doorway, the governess stepped out. She saw Mirabel and her face went pink.

"I'm afraid you can't see her today," the woman told Mirabel.

Mirabel stared, surprised. "Excuse me?"

"Master John left explicit instructions."

Mirabel stood and stared. It took a moment for the realization to trickle in. He'd forbidden the servants from letting her see her own child. He clearly wasn't going to give in as easily as he had before. But she knew she could not give in either.

So Mirabel didn't protest. She nodded to the governess, who looked relieved there wouldn't be a confrontation, and left. The walk through the gardens took longer than normal. There was nothing else for Mirabel to do.

She ate alone, spent her days alone and her nights. Since John's declaration, Mirabel hadn't slept in their marital bed. She'd retrieved clothes from their shared wardrobe and effectively moved back into her childhood room. Though it was strange, and a little lonely, Mirabel didn't mind too much. There was nothing she could do.

After that first day, Mirabel didn't try to see her daughter again. She saw no point in making an effort when it would only be rebuffed. And being forbidden from seeing the child removed a weight from her shoulders as well.

One night, Mirabel woke up, breath shuddering in her chest, to find John looming over her, a shadow in the night. She stifled a scream when she recognized him. His hand was outstretched and hovered in between them.

"John?"

"Mirabel," he stuttered. "I… I don't like this," he said, collapsing on the bed next to her.

"I don't either," she said, knowing that was what he wanted to hear.

"Then just give it up," he cried. "It's just a locket."

"It's not," Mirabel told him. "It's a part of me. I need it. You can ask anything of me but this."

He hung his head, the moon only touching his cheekbones. Mirabel reached up, unhappy to see him brought so low. He kissed the palm of her hand and nodded.

"You can have this," he said raggedly.

"Good. Then come to bed."

Mirabel made space in her childhood bed for her husband. It was not made for two adults, but they made do, clinging to one another. John rested his head on her chest, his breath stirring the frills of her nightclothes.

"I wish I could understand," he said, his fingers tracing the length of chain that held the locket.

Mirabel stroked the hair back from his forehead. She felt sleep tug at her awareness.

"I wish I could help you," she responded, her words slow and drawn out.

"If only I knew what it was about the locket," he said, sounding far too awake. His fingers wound around the locket, not actually touching. "Too much of you still remains a mystery. If I could see inside, perhaps then, I might understand."

"You would not like what you would find inside," Mirabel said.

"How do you know?" John asked, propping himself up to stare down at her.

Her eyes were half-lidded, drooping even as she watched him. "I know."

"Let me just look," he begged.

Mirabel shook her head. "No. I told you, it cannot be opened." She refused to give up the pretense that it could not be opened.

"Can it not? Or do you refuse to open it?" he asked, no longer looking at her but staring at the locket as the moonlight illuminated it.

"Both," she told him, starting to become worried. She tugged at him, trying to get him to lay down once more.

He refused to be budged. In a moment, he grabbed her wrists, holding them down. Mirabel cried out and struggled, tossing herself against him as she realized what he meant to do. John collapsed on her, his body weighing hers down. She still thrashed, crying out.

"John! Don't, John!"

"I'm doing this for you, Mirabel," he said through gritted teeth as he held her down.

His hand scrabbled for the locket, hoisting it aloft with a grunt of triumph. Mirabel's left hand twisted free in the distraction and she thumped him across the head with her closed fist. John swore and dropped the locket, hiking his body up just enough to pin her arms down under his thighs.

Thrashing, Mirabel howled as John once again grabbed the locket. He tried to pull it from the chain but it wouldn't break. Mirabel felt the chain rub and break the skin on her neck. Blood dripped onto the mattress below. Trying to wriggle loose, she couldn't take her eyes from John and what he held in her hand.

"It'll be ok, Mirabel. You'll see," John muttered as he stroked the locket.

"You're killing me, John," Mirabel moaned, wrenching her shoulders despite the pain of it.

"This is best for all of us," John told her.

And he stuck a fingernail in the edge of the locket and yanked it open. Mirabel screamed, her body lifting off the bed beneath them, sending John tumbling over the side. The locket slipped from his grasp.

John grabbed his ears with his hands, trying to shut out the shrieking cry coming from his wife. Mirabel's body shook once more then fell still and silent with a final shudder. The locket laid open on her chest, blood gushing from it. The blood stained her white nightclothes, running over the sides of her body to the sheets, dripping in little droplets on the floor.

John stared, unbelieving. There was something wet running down the side of his face. He wiped at it with one hand, pulling the hand away to see what it was. There was blood all over his hand. Both of his hands.

The locket was still bleeding, blood seeping slowly. It looked as though he'd ripped a hole in Mirabel's chest, though all he'd done was open the locket. John whimpered, pressing a slick hand to the side of his wife's neck.

There was no pulse, no heat left in her body. The white skin was cooling, her eyes open and unseeing, her mouth gaping in a fixed expression of horror. John gathered her to him, pulling her body over the side of the bed to drape across his lap on the floor.

"Mirabel?"

There was no answer. Her blood was hot against his nightclothes, soaking him. He shook her body, uncomprehendingly. Her head lolled on her neck.

"Mirabel?"

Her eyes didn't meet his. They stared at the ceiling, her face frozen. John snapped the locket closed, crushing it in one hand.

"I closed it, Mirabel. I put it back," he pleaded. "Wake up, Mirabel. I didn't know. I didn't know, Mirabel," he cried, hot tears pouring down his cheeks to mix with the blood smeared across both of them.

That was how Sarah found them the next morning, her scream alerting the household and sending two more servants running down the hallway to see what was wrong. The three of them froze in the doorway, afraid to enter even to see if either one of them was still alive. Neither of the bodies moved on the floor, even at Sarah's strangled whimper.

The two were intertwined, Mirabel draped across John's lap, her head cradled against his shoulder. Her nightgown was red, blood staining the pristine white. Mirabel's arms were flung out, splashes of red marring the white of her skin. Death hung over the room, though whose, the servants couldn't quite be sure.

Mistakes of the Mother

Mirabel sobbed on the front steps of the house, reaching after the horse galloping away.

"Daddy!"

Carolina pressed harder against one of the stone columns, hoping that it would steady her. Mirabel's cries tore at Carolina but there was nothing she could do. Mirabel was too young to understand that her precious Daddy didn't love them anymore. He hadn't for a while now.

Mirabel's teddy lay forgotten on the step below her while Mirabel cried, her face blotchy and wet. Carolina couldn't look at the dust thrown up by the horse's hooves or her husband's retreating back. It was easier to focus on Mirabel.

"Mira, come back into the house," Carolina heard herself say.

The three-year-old wouldn't move so Carolina picked her daughter up. Mirabel fought, scrabbling at her mother's arms, screaming for her daddy. Carolina evaded the wildly waving hands, carting her child back into the house. The two remaining servants watched, their faces pinched.

"Can you fetch her teddy, please?" Carolina asked, not looking at either of them. She knew what they were thinking and she had to hold herself together. Carolina could feel herself shredding away at the edges and knew it wouldn't be long before she collapsed, screaming and crying just like her three-year-old.

She managed to get Mirabel tucked up into her bed, her teddy in her arms. The girl cried herself to sleep while Carolina sat on the floor, terrified and lost.

Tomorrow wouldn't be any better. It would only get worse. Carolina knew because that was how it was when she'd first discovered her husband's indiscretions. This time, though, he'd hurt Mirabel. But Carolina could fix that. Out of anything, that, she could fix.

So when Mirabel looked as peaceful as she ever would, face mottled and swollen, Carolina did what she promised she never would. She climbed the stairs to the attic, where the pieces of her parents still remained.

The dark wooden desk sat where it had been put years ago. It was still swaddled in shadows, shadows the candlelight didn't even seem to want to touch. Carolina couldn't see it until she stood inches away though she didn't need to. Its dark energy pulled her towards it, as did her memory of the thing.

One of the locked drawers popped open at her touch. Carolina couldn't remember reaching in and pulling out the leather journal but suddenly it was in her hands. It fell open as it used to for her mother. Caroline had never opened it before.

The ritual and the words were laid out in front of her like a recipe for scones she once remembered making with her mother. It looked simple, requiring nothing she didn't have. In the morning, Carolina would have to find her brother, Albert, and give up what was left of her life. But tonight, she would do what she must to protect Mirabel. Albert would never approve or let her do such a thing under his roof. It had to be done now.

Her mother's jewelry box sat on an oaken wardrobe shelf. It held nothing of value, just pieces of sentiment that Albert had sent her when their mother died. The locket gravitated towards her touch, the chain wrapping around her fingers, tangling.

It was dark when Carolina navigated the stairs downwards. She hadn't taken a candle, afraid someone would see the light. The house sat silently, as if holding its breath.

Her thoughts were oddly clear. Everything else was blurry but the purpose she held in her mind.

Mirabel was still sleeping, clutching tightly to the teddy her daddy had bought before she'd been born. Carolina could remember the blue bow it used to have tied around its neck, now long since discarded.

Her daughter stirred at Carolina's footsteps. The moonlight poured through the window, painting Mirabel's face white. She didn't wake. Carolina blew out the candle that was always kept burning in her daughter's room. The crescent moon lit the scene with no trouble, stars absent from the sky.

It was too dark to read in Mirabel's room but she held the book open. The locket was cold in one hand, slick from her sweaty palm. There was still a chance to walk away but the wet cheeks of her daughter spurred her on.

The torn organ stuttering in Carolina's chest ached in sympathy and pumped in jealousy. It would remain untouched, a reminder of her mistakes. But they would remain her mistakes alone.

Reaching down, Carolina opened the throat of her daughter's dress, laying the girl bare to the breastbone. She laid the cold locket on the flesh there and Mirabel whimpered at the chill. Carolina hushed her, pausing to be sure Mirabel was still sleeping.

Pressing the locket down hard, the words flowed out of Carolina. Her voice hissed from her, out of her control. Carolina's eyes pierced the darkness, staring down at Mirabel, watching the ritual as though she didn't perform it.

As the words grew more heated, Mirabel moaned, thrashing. Carolina pressed harder on the locket, pinning her daughter to the bed. Mirabel's eyes popped open and she let out a piercing shriek, her back bending, anguish embedded in her expression. Carolina sobbed but didn't stop.

Mirabel's scream went on and on, obscuring the words. Carolina chanted faster, pushing harder as tears dripped. The locket began to heat under her hand, writhing and filling. She felt a sucking and a small pop ended the ritual. Mirabel's screams died away, her chest heaving.

Slowly, the anguished expression slid away until Mirabel's face was blank. The locket chain slithered around Mirabel's neck until it was fastened, no sign of a clasp. Carolina brushed the locket from her daughter's chest. The flesh was smooth and unmarked, showing no signs of what had happened.

"Mirabel?"

"Tired," Mirabel said with a yawn. She flung her teddy away and rolled over, tucking her legs up to her chest. She was asleep moments later.

Carolina stumbled backwards until her legs met the edge of a chair. The journal hung from her hand as though it was attached. The pages fluttered, pleased. Carolina flung it away from her with an oath.

It was done and she would never have to touch the book again. Mirabel could live her own life at the behest of no one else. She could make her own mistakes. She had no opportunity to repeat her mother's now. Her heart would be forever protected in a shell of gold.

The Amaranthine Dowager

The Dowager stood at the window, waiting, her eyes straining for a glimpse of the carriages. In her left hand she clutched the letter from Clementine, giving the date of her arrival. Luncheon had been laid for an hour or more by now without any guests to enjoy it.

Around the time that her feet began to truly ache, a blur on the horizon started to resemble two horses. The Dowager stood there until she was certain. The heavy fall of fabric closed behind her as she turned to hurry across the room, a small smile engraved on her face.

By the time she'd alerted the staff and made it to the top of the stairs, the door was breached. Clementine's family was still young and the two boys fell through the opening, clambering into the echoing foyer. When they saw her, they shouted, scrambling up the stairs.

The Dowager collected them to her and pressed them into her skirts. Their hair was fine as down as she ran her fingers through it. They grinned up eagerly at her, remembering her from past visits.

"A long trip?" she asked over their rambunctious hellos.

They fought to tell her of their many adventures on the road. The Dowager listened with one ear, the other listening to Clementine's murmured responses to her husband.

"A meal is waiting for you in the dining hall, if you can find it," the Dowager told the two boys.

They took the hint and ran off, spinning a servant in place as they galloped past her. The Dowager only spared the woman a glance to make sure she was still on her feet.

Then she was trying not to hurry down the stairs while Clementine and her husband watched. Smiling, she held her arms out to Clementine when her feet hit the floor. Clementine shifted the bundle in her arms, which murmured, and clasped the Dowager.

"Lady Althea," Clementine's husband said in greeting once the Dowager had disentangled from Clementine.

"Albert," the Dowager responded. "Thank you for bringing your family to visit. I have a meal prepared if you are hungry from your journey."

Albert would not give her a moment alone with Clementine and her new baby. Instead, he paced them all the way to the dining hall and sat at her side when they arrived.

The Dowager forbore to say anything. Albert was a necessary evil for spending time with her Clementine.

They ate slowly, lingering over the food and conversation. The boys grew restless, as did the baby, and the Dowager turned to Albert and instructed him to take them from the table. He glowered at her but did as she requested.

"We'll retire to the library, Clemmy," the Dowager said.

Clementine flushed and laughed to be called Clemmy once more. "No one calls me that any longer, Mother," she reminded the Dowager.

"And no one calls me Mother but you," the Dowager responded. It was a misnomer in more ways than one.

The walk to the library was paved in lush carpets and wood paneling. The Dowager asked after Clementine's health, as well as the baby's.

"We're both doing well. She was easier than the boys," Clementine replied. "Everything about her has been easier."

"Perhaps because she is your third."

"Perhaps."

The library was flooded with late afternoon sun and the two women sat in front of the large windows that showed the gardens and the land beyond. Tea was waiting for them as the servants were well used to the structure of these visits. They'd been with the Dowager for many years.

"And how is Albert getting on?" the Dowager made herself ask.

Clementine shot her an amused glance. "Well enough, though he wishes we would visit you more."

"I wish the same. You and the children are welcome to come stay with me for the summer."

"He would willingly allow us to trouble you for any length of time," Clementine said, sounding distant. There was a hard shell over her eyes and she looked away from the Dowager, out the window.

"It has been some time since I've spoken to Albert alone," the Dowager commented, also enjoying the view.

"There is nothing for the two of you to speak of."

"We share you in common," the Dowager said. Clementine gave a bleak laugh. The Dowager paused before saying, "You needn't stay with him."

Clementine merely took a sip of her tea and a bite of a biscuit. "He's good for the children."

"They would be happy here." The Dowager didn't need to mention that she would also be happier with them under her roof.

"What would the rest of grandfather's children and grand-children think of such an arrangement," Clementine asked, a small glint of amusement in her expression.

The Dowager smirked. "They would think you were a favorite and they would be correct."

Clementine shook her head, her soft dress susurrating against the velvet upholstery of the divan at the movement. "Neither of us could bear to give them facts to such an assumption."

"True. I am not quite ready to go yet," the Dowager replied. "And I know they would plague me mercilessly if I promised the inheritance to you before my death bed."

The Dowager surveyed her step-granddaughter over the rim of her teacup, assessing. Clementine was much older now. A little too old for another child but maybe wiser.

"Are you interested in the inheritance," the Dowager asked, weary of dancing around the subject. Though she wasn't ready to go, as she'd said, it would be nice to have it arranged. One less weight on her shoulders.

Clementine reddened. "I think it would be too much for me and even for Albert, though he wouldn't be happy to hear me say it. I don't even know all that it encompasses."

"No, you don't. But I would be willing to share the details with you. However, it would be yours, not Albert's."

Clementine frowned at that, her fingers twisting in her lap. "I think now isn't the time to mention it. Besides, you've hardly aged at all since Grandfather died. I think there are many years left for you."

The Dowager inclined her head with a small smile. It was truer than Clementine knew but she made no comment. Clementine didn't have to say it any clearer, that she didn't want the inheritance. It would be a burden to her, which the Dowager understood. She had a long life with her family ahead of her.

Gracefully changing the subject back to Clementine's children, the Dowager settled more firmly in her seat, soaking in the pleasant atmosphere. It was rare that she enjoyed a visit from family and even rarer that she only had one family to contend with.

The visit lasted too short a time, as Clementine's visits always did. And once the rest of the family heard about her visit alone, the Dowager was descended upon by the hordes. For three months, the Dowager did nothing but entertain. It was a steep price for the week with Clementine though she paid it willingly.

When an heir didn't seem forthcoming and Clementine was not confirmed as such, the visits trickled to an end. With the deluge finished, the Dowager was given time to return to her part in managing the vast estate she'd inherited. This was time consuming and stressful in its own ways but she was well used to it now, with her husband dead twenty years.

It took Clementine another three years to arrange an excursion to the Dowager's abode. This time, Albert did not accompany her, her mother did. Clementine's mother was one of the few remaining children.

The boys were older and not as prone to displays of affection. They were shy with the Dowager, standing straight but slightly behind their mother and grandmother, as though afraid. The young daughter was the only one not frightened.

She was happy to toddle into the Dowager's outstretched arms under her grandmother's watchful eye. The Dowager ignored Bienda, concentrating on the child in her arms.

"How have you been, sweetling? I haven't seen you since you were a tiny baby," the Dowager cooed.

"Her name is Clementha," Bienda scowled.

The Dowager didn't look up at her step-daughter. Bienda had come from the third wife, her middle daughter. She'd never had a honeyed disposition and it was a wonder Clementine had turned out so well.

"Clementha isn't a name suitable for such a small child, is it, sweetling?" the Dowager asked the girl in her arms.

Clementha giggled and tugged on the broach at the Dowager's throat. She didn't reply to the question, more than happy with her occupation.

"No, I think I'll call you Clemmy Two instead."

Out of the corner of her eye, the Dowager caught Bienda's look of horror and Clementine's grin. Clementha seemed pleased and repeated her new name carefully with the Dowager's encouragement.

The visit did not go as smoothly as it would have done, had Clementine arrived alone. As the Dowager expected, Bienda caught her more than once alone. The conversation rarely varied.

"I hope you're still looking to Father's children for an heir," Bienda started.

It was one of her less subtle openings and the Dowager sighed internally, waiting for the rest of it. She'd been cornered in the library, uncertain how Bienda had even known where to find her in the vast manor. She hoped her servants weren't giving her away, they'd been given detailed instructions on the family.

"There aren't too many of you left," the Dowager observed. Of the original eight children, only four of them remained.

Bienda reacted as though she'd been slapped. The Dowager stared at her, surprised. Both of Bienda's sisters were still alive and she'd never been close with any of her half-brothers and sisters.

"Still," Bienda said, recovering. "It shouldn't miss a generation."

"It missed a generation for your father," the Dowager reminded Bienda. The woman didn't enjoy that being pointed out. "This family hardly seems to follow the conventions for inheritance and I have complete freedom in that respect."

The Dowager fully enjoyed being taller than average. She peered down her nose at Bienda. The third wife had birthed three daughters, all frail, wispy things with an annoying amount of vinegar running through their veins.

"I'm not quite ready to die yet," the Dowager said, repeating the phrase she was growing sick of. It was used at least once a visit with any of the family.

Bienda flushed, surprising the Dowager. She didn't think the woman had enough shame to blush, even at her eagerness for a relative's death.

"Even if I was, would you really fault the generational gap if the inheritance was to go to your daughter?" The Dowager asked, curious.

There was no immediate answer and the Dowager continued to stare at her step-daughter, who was almost as old as the Dowager looked. She was uncertain how long the woman would last without replying to the direct question.

Finally, Bienda snapped, "It just isn't proper."

The Dowager allowed herself a chuckle. "And I'm sure the whole family thinks it isn't proper that I received the inheritance at all."

It was a statement, nothing more but she could see the embarrassment it caused Bienda. It was far too accurate, the Dowager was certain.

"Just be glad I didn't have children to favor," the Dowager told her step-daughter. At moments like these she was forever grateful that she'd managed to elude motherhood.

The visit didn't last as long as the Dowager hoped it might. She could never tell how long it would be before she saw Clementine again. But she pushed aside the thought and went back to her daily life.

But irritated by Bienda's audacity, the Dowager was less giving when the first wife's family arrived a mere two weeks after Clementine's departure.

Laticia was a doppelganger for her grandmother, the first wife, well over sixty years deceased. The Dowager had never known the first wife, she'd never known any of them, but her husband kept paintings of each one hanging in the main hall. Even so long after their deaths, including her husband's, the Dowager had yet to remove them.

As the eldest grandchild, Laticia felt entitled. This attitude soured her and she'd never liked the latest wife, whom she felt had encroached upon the family and had never really become part of it.

The Dowager couldn't decide if Laticia visited out of a sense of obligation or out of spite. Surely the woman knew she wouldn't receive the inheritance, though she felt it was her due. No matter the reason, the results were the same. Unpleasantness.

Laticia always visited with her younger brother and at least two children. If it had been anyone else perhaps the Dowager would have behaved slightly differently. No warning had been issued for their arrival so when the Dowager was interrupted in her study with the news, she balked at politeness.

"Sit them in the far receiving room," the Dowager told her husband's manservant.

He nodded and didn't question her. Though her husband had been dead around twenty years now, she kept all of his servants employed. They all came from one family into which loyalty and discretion were bred.

Embroiled in tricky estate affairs, the Dowager quickly forgot her troublesome visitors. Two hours later her husband's manservant knocked again.

All it took was a look at his face to remind her. Straightening with a flush, the Dowager put down the papers she'd been perusing.

"Have Christine put on a tea for them if she hasn't already. Use the guest china and see if the kitchen can put together some tarts. I'll be down in a bit."

Though putting off the confrontation would only compound the issue, the Dowager wanted time to finish her work and compose herself. Both took longer than she expected and almost another hour passed before she left her study.

She refused to feel remorse or guilt as she sedately wandered in the direction of the receiving room she'd requested they be placed in.

The tea was gone and the plates empty when the Dowager opened the door. Laticia's back was to her, her spine straight and her shoulders tense. Her youngest children, and two of Roger's children, gathered on the couches, their faces pinched. Roger was ignoring everyone, his gaze fixed out the window.

"Laticia, Roger, I wasn't expecting you," the Dowager said into the thick silence. She stood a few feet in front the doorway but didn't sit.

"Yes, it does seem you had much to keep you from your guests," Laticia finally said, her tone icy.

"I inherited a large estate, the running of which takes up almost all of my time. I would hate to be accused of allowing it to flounder to the detriment of my heir."

Laticia startled at that. None of the family realized everything that went into the running of the estate or indeed, how much work it really was. The Dowager was not an idle woman of means.

Roger's gaze finally came into the room once more. "I apologize for not sending word of our visit, Dowager," the man said. His words were distant as everything about him was. It was as though he'd wilted and shrunk to fit inside his older sister's shadow. The Dowager had only met his wife once, on their wedding day.

The Dowager inclined her head, feeling it bowed by social niceties. "Thank you for the apology. It really is an inconvenient time, I am afraid."

"Clementine was just here," Laticia retorted. "You had time for her visit, I assume."

"Yes, they warned me two months in advance and I accommodated them into my work schedule as best I could." The Dowager wouldn't be flustered by Laticia's snide insinuations. "I hope the refreshments were to your taste," she said instead, nodding at the elegant tea set sitting on a side table.

"The blackberry tart was delicious," one of the children said from the couch. Two of the faces had a purple tinge to them and the Dowager allowed herself to smile.

"I'll be glad to relay your appreciation to the kitchen," the Dowager told them. "Now, I'm afraid I must return to my work. Your rooms are set up as usual but I'm afraid I'll have to ask you to stay away from the third floor of the manor. It's being redone."

Turning with a slick swish of her dress, the Dowager headed for the hallway, hoping to get away without any fuss.

Laticia called after her. "When will we be graced with your presence again?" There was something of a sneer in her voice.

"I will join you for dinner at seven," the Dowager said over her shoulder.

She escaped to her study with a sigh. Putting Laticia off would only last so long, as she knew from past experience. The woman would have her visit and she would impinge on the Dowager no matter how the Dowager protested her busyness.

Laticia and her brother stayed two weeks. By the end of it, the Dowager was fed up and frustrated. Once they'd left she vowed to refuse all visits for the next six months. If she'd had a smaller family, perhaps yearly or bi-yearly visits wouldn't be so taxing but with three separate families, there seemed to be guests every month.

The Dowager's social life consisted of her family's visits and her business dealings. It was a sad state of affairs at times. At the end of her six month embargo on family, the Dowager found herself disconsolate, lonely without dinner conversation or evening companionship.

Her husband had warned her of the life she could expect with him. Even after he died, the Dowager continued to live as she had while he'd been alive. It was due to this enforced isolation that her husband decided to have a large family, for company.

His predecessor had had the requisite heir and spare and then promptly retreated from his family. He'd only reemerged to pick his heir, as this family often didn't pass the inheritance linearly, and then expired. Her husband had been left with little information or preparation and an estate.

Sitting at her vanity, the Dowager stared at herself in the ornate looking glass. She looked much younger than her years. With her collar open at the throat, her brooch in front of her, she could see the dim blue glow of her pendant.

Peeling back the satin fabric further, the Dowager leaned forward, the amulet flopping out of her bodice. It lit her pink shirt lilac. Reaching up, she fingered it, letting it roll over her palm.

The Dowager sighed and loosed it. Not for the first time she wondered at the direction her life had taken. She'd never expected to be a fourth wife or to have stumbled into the wealth she now possessed. She'd also expected to have children.

Now she was a widow with a long life ahead of her. She missed her husband, even so long after his death. Though she'd thought she'd spend her twilight years in idleness or traveling, instead she was mired in the business of running a vast estate.

She'd surprised herself with her aptitude and her enjoyment of it all. Her first four decades of life had been concerned with frivolity. No longer.

It was a wonder she'd been chosen for the inheritance. The Dowager was hardly the only one who thought it had been an oversight, though she'd proven herself capable. Handling responsibility or money had never been her forte but now it was her life.

With a sigh, the Dowager wiped her hand over her reflection as if to wipe it away. She was merely lonely and it made her introspective. Six months was a long time without visitors.

Straightening, she eyed herself again. The Dowager tucked away the pendant, dimming the glow. Tomorrow she would invite Clementine for a visit. And maybe some of the other family. The melancholia had to end. She was too young to go the way of her husband.

Enclosed in the soft darkness of her overly large bed, the Dowager found sleep easy for the first time in weeks. In the morning she sent out invitations for all of the family, staggering arrival dates so that she would have a pleasantly full, but not overwhelming, schedule for the next six months.

Everyone answered their invitation in the affirmative. It was rare that the Dowager would issue one. Distantly she hoped that no one was expecting an announcement.

Unfortunately, the family did expect something after a rare invitation. They all went home disappointed. However, the visits had been much more pleasant than normal with everyone well behaved.

Clementine's visit had been pushed back due to Albert's schedule. He hadn't been able to get away from the law office for quite some time after their invitation date. The Dowager wrote to say that Clementine and the children were welcome to come alone. Albert wrote a terse reply, saying that he would be accompanying his family in November. The Dowager sighed as she read the letter but didn't argue.

When the family did arrive, something felt different. She couldn't say what it was but it made her wary. The children were the same, though older. The difference was Albert or Clementine or the dynamic between the two of them.

The Dowager didn't address the issue, unsure of how to. She was certain that in time she would understand or be told of some change. When it happened, she was surprised.

Albert arranged to be away with the children, giving the Dowager an afternoon with Clementine. Normally he made this quite difficult and she had to insist. It put her on guard to be given what she wanted with no fuss and to be accommodated by Albert of all people.

Clementine also looked mildly uncomfortable. Because of this, the Dowager took Clementine up to her suite of rooms and sat the woman in her lounge. It was no trouble to have the tea redirected and Clementine looked slightly more at ease. There was nothing for it and the Dowager sat across from her step-granddaughter and waited.

Nothing was said until the tea had arrived and the woman who brought it had left. The Dowager gave Clementine time to stall by letting her bother over their teacups and refreshments. But it seemed that Clementine wasn't going to tell the Dowager anything.

"What is it?" the Dowager eventually had to ask in a firm voice.

Clementine started, shaking the teacup in her hand so that it clinked and spilled a little of the honey-colored liquid onto the saucer.

"Oh!" Clementine said, grabbing a napkin to dab at it.

"Clemmy, it's fine. Stop it. Tell me what is bothering you. Is it Albert?" She didn't enjoy being blunt like this with Clementine who didn't always respond well to it but there was nothing else to do at this point.

Clementine looked up, her yellow dress making her look paler. Placing her teacup down, rattling it, she folded her hands in her lap, clenching them together. Her lips were pressed together, white around the edges.

The Dowager felt her face crease, worried. She'd never seen Clementine in such a state.

"What is it?" she pressed, trying to keep the urgency out of her voice.

"Albert- I- I'd be happy to be your heir." Clementine didn't look convinced of her own words.

The Dowager gave her a hard look. Albert's name was not unexpected when mentioning the inheritance. Though Laticia felt entitled, her greed could never rival Albert's.

"Do you remember me telling you that it would be you and not Albert that would receive the inheritance, Clemmy?"

Clementine bobbed her head, her eyes stuck on the Dowager's face, wide.

The Dowager shifted on her blue couch. "Are you sure? You don't look very sure."

Clementine nodded again, looking slightly surer. Or at least resolute.

Cocking her own head, the Dowager surveyed the woman in front of her. "What do you think the inheritance is comprised of? Tell me your expectations." She was interested to hear what Clementine would say.

Clementine blanched, her eyes taking a moment to glaze, an indication that she was thinking. The Dowager waited patiently.

"I suppose it's money, land, businesses. Things of those nature."

The Dowager restrained an unladylike snort at the naïve and ambiguous answer. Clementine had been raised to be a proper lady. She shouldn't know what to expect and the part of the inheritance which the Dowager thought Clementine was uniquely suited for wasn't part of the rest of the dealings. Clementine could learn business and money as the Dowager had done.

"Am I wrong," Clementine asked when the Dowager didn't immediately comment.

"Not entirely," she prevaricated.

Though she'd though about this conversation many times before, it was still difficult to know where to begin. "There's more to it than that."

Clementine smiled unexpectedly. "I hope so. I'm not much for business."

"That's not why I've offered it to you," the Dowager smiled back, reaching over the small space between them to pat Clementine's hands, still gathered together. "There's something to it that's much more important." She paused, uncertain how to continue.

"Well?" Clementine asked, leaning forward. Her expression was confused between several emotions, making the Dowager smile in sympathy.

"I'm sure you've heard the stories, the rumors about this family. About your grandfather."

Shifting on the couch, Clementine frowned. There were a multitude of stories and rumors and likely she wasn't sure which ones the Dowager meant.

The Dowager sighed. Reaching up, she unclasped her necktie, unbuttoning her high collar. Clementine looked uncomfortable but didn't stop watching, rapt. The frown reappeared when the blue glow became obvious.

The Dowager pulled out the necklace, dangling on a thin silver chain. She held it in her hand, holding it so that Clementine could see it clearly. While the woman stared, the Dowager told her of the inheritance. Of what it would mean and what Clementine could truly expect.

As she spoke, she watched Clementine's expression shift slowly, from blank to horror. But still, she spoke, hoping that at some point, Clementine would show some interest, even a glimmer, to work with. It never appeared.

Eventually, the Dowager ran out of words to say and she let her hand fall back into her lap, the amulet to bounce against her breast bone and settle on top of the soft linen, glowing. She waited for Clementine, hoping that her expression was not an indication of how the rest of the conversation would go.

"That? That is what you want for me?" Clementine eventually asked, horrified, her eyes gleaming. "Grandfather was… he couldn't have been happy and what a… what a life to lead."

"He led a good life," the Dowager said, defending her husband. "He never did wrong intentionally and he was happy."

Clementine shook her head, her hands clasped even tighter in her lap. The Dowager could see them faintly trembling.

"He left the inheritance to me, for me to pass on," the Dowager said. "I've waited to find someone who would do well with it. Could you imagine Laticia with such an inheritance? Or Albert?"

The words didn't seem to strike Clementine as the Dowager had meant them to.

The Dowager tried again. "It is my responsibility to find the right person but I have no intention of giving it over so soon. I am still young and you would have time, more than enough time, with me to learn what you need to learn, to become accustomed-"

"Accustomed!" Clementine cut her off with a sharp bark of laughter. "Accustomed! How could one become accustomed to such… travesty? Such blasphemy! All the time in the world couldn't-" She choked on the words, stumbling to a stop. Her face was pale, devoid of any color.

"You can become accustomed to anything," the Dowager replied. She stood, walking to the window to give them both some space and distance. "I was surprised, like you, though perhaps less so. I'd lived with your grandfather for years before he told me. By then, I already knew something was amiss."

"Amiss? Unnatural, more like," Clementine retorted.

There was more spirit in her voice than the Dowager had heard in a long time. Since she'd married Albert, perhaps.

"The inheritance is a whole," the Dowager told her. "It cannot be split. You cannot take what you will from it and leave the rest."

"I said no the last time you offered," Clementine reminded her.

"Yes, I remember. But here you are, at your husband's behest, I assume." She didn't have to turn and look to imagine the face Clementine wore. It would be ashamed. "But it doesn't matter. None of it can be his and I would not give it to you until he was gone."

"I don't want it," Clementine said into the silence following the Dowager's announcement.

"You have time to change your mind."

"I won't change my mind. You'll have to find someone else."

The Dowager didn't reply. She was certain that Clementine would give in. After all, the Dowager had given in eventually, though she'd never expected to see the inheritance for different reasons.

Clementine didn't stay much longer after that and it was the last time she spent alone with the Dowager. The visit was cut short. This time, it was Clementine who prompted their return home, though it could have easily been Albert.

The Dowager assumed that Clementine told him the inheritance wasn't going to be his. He'd been followed by a black cloud as he stalked about the floors. It was relief to see him go, though the Dowager was sad to say goodbye to the children. She enjoyed children for their simplicities and complexities.

Another year passed, then another. Clementine had an excuse for every visit she didn't make. Albert was busy, the children were sick. But the Dowager continued to send invitations. And they were declined again and again.

It took five years for the rest of the family to realize that Clementine had stopped visiting entirely. The Dowager could feel their glee in their renewed attempts to court her. It made for a depressing time. But the Dowager waited, certain that Clementine would come to her senses. It was a lot to take in, to accept.

On the sixth year of their estrangement, Clementine's children arrived with their uncle. Sensing a thaw in the rift, the Dowager welcomed them more effusively than before.

With five years between visits, the boys had become young men, uncertain of her. Clementha was also uncertain, though why, the Dowager did not know. Clementine wasn't the sort to poison a relationship with hurtful words and Albert wasn't the kind to spend time with his children.

It took a week for Clementha to muster the courage to approach the Dowager. And the Dowager learned of her great-grandchild's hesitancy.

"Grandmother?"

The Dowager put down the book she'd been reading. They were alone in the library but she looked around anyway, wondering who had escorted the child this deep into the house.

"Why do they call you the Amaranthine Dowager," Clementha asked. She stepped further into the room so that she was only a few feet from the Dowager. Her eyes were wide as she stared up at her step-great-grandmother.

The Dowager's eyes widened, then narrowed. Sweeping the room with her gaze once more, she wondered if she should call out. It would be just like Clementha's older brothers to play a prank of this nature. She could almost predict how it would go.

The Dowager leaned over the velvet-padded arm of her chair to look into Clementha's eyes.

"Is that what they call me?"

The little girl nodded, her wild hair escaping from the neat braid her mother had tamed it into. Earnestness was written on her face.

"It's a joke," the Dowager said, relenting.

"It doesn't sound funny. What does amaranthine mean?"

"It means undying. Who did you hear this from?"

Eyes wide and bright, Clementha bit her lip before answering. "People."

"People?"

Clementha nodded, her hair catching the sun's light and glittering. "Lots of people."

"Lots of people," the Dowager repeated, incredulous.

"Aunties and uncles," Clementha expounded. "And some cousins," her face wrinkled at that as though she didn't like her cousins. "And it means undying?"

"Yes."

Clementha's face scrunched further at that. "Huh," she grunted as though she was trying to puzzle something out. "Undying like you can't die?"

"That's what it means," the Dowager said, bending her head in a nod. "But they mean it as a joke because they want the inheritance and I just won't die and give it to them."

Clementha's eyes widened and she looked horrified. "They want you to die?" she whispered hoarsely.

Her words and the look on her face made the Dowager regret her bluntness. She didn't know what to say. Clementha stumbled towards the Dowager, reaching out to grab as much of her as she could.

"I don't want you to die. You aren't going to, are you?"

Placing a hand gently on the girl's head, the Dowager couldn't help feeling touched. "Not any time soon, Clemmy Two."

Clementha laughed. "I like that."

"I thought you might. A little better than Clementha?"

Clementha nodded, clinging tighter. "I like you more than my grandmother. She isn't as nice as you."

The feeling was mutual. The Dowager reveled in being around any of Clementine's family and her children were delightful. She hoped that they would take tales home with them and that Clementine would eventually come out of hiding.

But the next year, Clementine didn't come. She sent her children roughly every six months, always with a chaperone. Sometimes they came with their aunts or uncles, cousins in tow. Other times they came with their maternal grandparents.

The Dowager didn't mind who they came with. It was enough that they came, she tried to tell herself, ignoring the quickly beating heart when the carriage pulled up and the disappointment when Clementine didn't alight. Letters to Clementine were not answered though her children continued to visit.

After years without Clementine's presence, the Dowager began to really worry about the inheritance. Perhaps Clementine had spoken the truth the last time she'd visited. The thought was depressing.

The Dowager tried to comfort herself with the children's visits but she missed Clementine. She'd written numerous times, begging her to visit. She promised to never mention the inheritance again if that's what it took. But Clementine never came.

Eventually, she took to asking the rest of the family about Clementine. There was nothing else for it and the Dowager hoped someone was visiting her Clemmy. She even asked Dahlia, one of Clementine's aunts, to speak to her. But the woman came back with nothing to report.

On the eighth year, the Dowager decided to resort to something else entirely. She invited the whole family for Christmas. Normally the time was spent alone. But that year, the Dowager threw a large party for the whole family. They were all invited to stay for two weeks.

No one turned down the invitation. But Clementine's family was only represented by her children. She and Albert remained behind. Clementha said that her father's mother was ill but her eyes were troubled as though she'd just started to realize that her parents never came to visit.

But the Dowager was not one easily foiled. Every year she threw the same Christmas party, inviting Clementine just the same. Surprisingly, in hosting such a large family gathering, other unexpected visits throughout the year were cut down. And with so many people competing for her attention and favor, the Christmas party was never dull. Often far too competitive and spiteful, but never dull. This year, the Dowager did not look forward to the familiar dance of family politics.

The Dowager stood at the window. She twitched aside the filmy curtain so that she could look down at the carriages arriving. Laticia and Roger. Squinting, she thought she saw Bienda's carriage following behind. They were early this year.

She stepped away from the window once she was certain they'd seen her silhouette. The Dowager was a little surprised to see her husband's oldest daughter's carriage.

"Lady Althea, they've arrived. Would you like to greet them in the Red Receiving Room?"

"Of course," she replied. This visit would be no different than any other. Even if it was premature. Most of the house was still being decorated for the party which was still a few days away.

By the time her step-family was at the double doors of the receiving room, the Dowager was already installed in her chair. It sat above the ground on a squat pedestal, throne-like.

She waited for the families to enter. They each kissed her cheek, murmuring hellos before they sat. The Dowager surveyed them with cold eyes. It had already been a bad day, after a distressing letter from Clementha and a business deal gone sour. And she didn't like surprises.

Laticia was the first to break the silence. "How have you been, Mother?"

"I'm surprised you managed to make it," the Dowager replied snidely, not addressing the erroneous title of 'Mother'. Laticia knew how she felt about that, it was a slap in the face to hear it from Laticia. Clementine was the only one who ever called her that. "Where is Clemmy?"

The question had been directed at Bienda. The Dowager knew it made her look weak and foolish but she couldn't stop herself from asking. Someday, she hoped the answer would be different.

Laticia reddened angrily, making her pale hair stand out even more. Roger fidgeted. His wife grabbed his hand.

"Clemmy refused to come," Bienda said. There was something of a smirk in her voice. The Dowager wondered at Bienda's attitude to her daughter.

"Refused?" the Dowager asked sharply. She hadn't expected Bienda to have spoken to Clementine. Bienda resented Clementine being the Dowager's favorite.

Laticia nodded. "She didn't want to see you again. I wish she would tell us why, but I suppose that's between the two of you." Her expression was sour. "Maybe she's unhappy with you dangling the inheritance in front of each of us in turn."

Roger's wife gasped, her face whitening. No one else made a sound. It was a bold statement, one that the children had been dancing around for years, since their father's death. Now the grandchildren joined in the waltz.

"I don't…*dangle*," the Dowager told Laticia in an icy voice. "You *assume* that one of you will be receiving it."

"He was our blood," Laticia fumed. "You were his fourth wife! Why should you get it? My mother went through life expecting that inheritance!"

"Your grandfather gave it to me, and the law," the Dowager informed her. "You may fight over the property when I am dead." Both statements were lies.

One of Laticia's middle-aged daughters snorted.

"You could at least share some of our grandfather's inheritance with us," Laticia said stiffly.

"I cannot. It is one inheritance. It cannot be split," the Dowager said, sick of repeating these same arguments over and over. Though they did not know the particulars of the inheritance, she knew what assumptions they made about it.

Dinner was not an improvement. Laticia's spite flavored every course. The grandchildren and great grandchildren that had accompanied her husband's children offered no respite. Once upon a time, the Dowager had enjoyed having children about the place, the one saving grace of these visit. But now, even the babies seemed to stare at her with greedy, beady eyes.

She retired as early as she could. They would all be there in the morning, ready to beset her anew. Everyone seemed to believe she'd outlived her welcome. Even the Dowager was starting to believe it.

The week passed slowly, as those weeks with the family always did. This Christmas felt worse than the ones before it. She felt trapped, afraid of being cornered by another relative barely related to her. Each thought they could threaten, cajole or win the inheritance from her.

The night they left, almost two weeks into the New Year, the Dowager sat at her vanity as she unclasped her jewelry, all gifts from her late husband. None were as valuable as the real inheritance he'd given her, though she was growing weary of it now.

"Althea," her husband had told her when he'd decided to die, "someday you'll realize why I'm doing this. There comes a point when there isn't life to live anymore."

She'd scoffed at him, feeling too young even in her forties and certain she'd never feel otherwise. Now, she'd realized he was right. Especially as her duties as Dowager weighed more on her each day. The responsibilities held no pleasure and with her husband dead, no family left of her own, the Dowager didn't see any reason to remain, except that she couldn't leave just yet.

"Maybe if I'd had children of my own," she muttered to herself in the mirror. But she'd never wanted any, enamored of the life she shared with her husband. Besides, he'd had more than enough for both of them. She shuddered at the thought of another gaggle of grown children, all harkening after the inheritance.

Clementine was the closest she had to a child and now the woman refused to visit her. Sighing, the Dowager wrapped her silk robe about her shoulders and went to bed.

The day after they left, she refused to get out of bed. Not even when someone knocked on the door. Her breakfast was left on its tray outside her door and was joined later by her lunch and dinner.

As had become normal now, the visits drained her and it took her longer and longer to recover, the older she got. By the time she was eating at a table again, she'd been warned of another onset of visitors.

The Dowager refused to ask who was to arrive. She knew it wouldn't be Clementine. Bienda had been eager to make that clear to her.

She took her time dressing. The plum-colored, high neck dress was intimidating and didn't make her look like a corpse. She gave orders for the visitors to be detained until she could make it down to the library.

The Dowager was too tired for the cold comforts of any of the receiving rooms. She collapsed on her favorite red velvet chair, the window at her back to shade her face. While she waited, she rested her head on her hand.

It wasn't until she heard the soft footsteps that she perked up. Straightening, she leaned backwards for much needed support. The door creaked open and the Dowager made a mental note to get the hinges oiled.

Clementha's wary face appeared in the opening. The Dowager relaxed, smiling and waving Clementine's daughter in. When Clementha saw the welcome on the Dowager's face, she smiled back and entered the room with less trepidation.

"Grandmother?"

"Clemmy Two," the Dowager said with a laugh. "I didn't expect it would be you when they said I was to have visitors. Are you alone?"

Clementha paused before nodding, taking a seat where the Dowager directed. Tea wouldn't be far behind.

"You seemed very sad this Christmas," Clementha said. "I told Mother. She was sad to hear it."

"Bienda said Clementine refused when she asked her to come."

Clementha shifted on the cushion. She was hiding something. "She's outside in the carriage. Laticia's been saying you looked like you were declining over the last three years. This was the worst and I... I thought maybe she was right."

"She's in the carriage?" The Dowager felt her heart beat stronger in her chest, some of the exhaustion leaving her. "Not coming in, though?"

Clementha shook her head as her hands tangled in her lap. "Sorry."

The Dowager grabbed Clementha's hand, pressing down on it. "It's my own fault."

"I doubt that, Grandmother. She's just afraid."

"Afraid?"

"Of wanting it."

"The inheritance." She'd offered it to Clemmy. But the woman was afraid of what it entailed, as she should have been. The Amaranth wasn't for everyone, though the Dowager hadn't realized she'd told Clementha about it.

Clementha nodded, her braid slithering around her neck to flop against her collarbone. "It's a lot of responsibility. And Mother... She... Father controls everything she does. I think she's afraid she wouldn't know what to do with it all."

The Dowager sunk back against the cushion. Clementha didn't know. She sighed.

"I'm not afraid."

Clementha's words startled her. The Dowager turned her head to stare at her. It suddenly occurred to her that Clementha was getting older.

"You aren't married," the Dowager commented with a little frown on her forehead.

Clementha startled and then blushed at the observation. She was certainly old enough to be married with a child of her own.

"No, I'm not," Clementha said. She ducked her head and looked up through her eyelashes. "Do you disapprove?"

It wasn't the response the Dowager had expected. She didn't see any shame in Clementha's expression.

"How can I disapprove?" the Dowager asked. "I've been a widow longer than I was married. I certainly never thought to remarry. And it's obvious I feel there's more to a woman's life than children and a husband."

Clementha seemed to deflate. She flopped back as much as her corset would allow, raking a hand over her neatly arranged hair.

"You're about the only one then," Clementha muttered.

The Dowager grinned at Clementha's sullen words. Albert must be a difficult father and it was strange that Clementha wasn't married. The thought weighed on her the more she ruminated.

"Is Albert pressuring you?"

"I've had four suitors," Clementha answered. "I didn't like any of them."

"I assumed your father wouldn't care your thoughts on them." As she said it, the Dowager realized it was an insensitive thing to say but she felt livelier than she had in a while.

"He doesn't but when the suitor removes his suit then there is nothing Father can do." Clementha smirked, showing a spirit that Clementine hadn't had for years.

"What do you want from your life?"

At that, Clementha paused. She didn't appear to have an answer ready. She frowned, her eyes glazing in imitation of her mother's thinking expression. It made the Dowager smile.

"I don't really know. I never thought beyond making sure I found someone I could live with. Someone who I wouldn't mind having children with."

"What if you could have more?"

It took seconds for Clementha to realize what the Dowager was asking. She took a long look at her great-grandmother as if testing her sincerity. The Dowager sat impassively and waited for it to be over.

"I thought you wanted my mother to have the inheritance," Clementha said slowly.

"She doesn't want it, as I'm sure she told you." This was where it would become more difficult. For the brief moment that the Dowager had thought Clementine had revealed the truth of the inheritance she'd been beset with relief.

"She said it would be too much for her," Clementha agreed with a nod. A wisp of hair escaped from her coif.

"I'm going to tell you about it and then you can return home with your mother. Think about it and if you decide you might like to be considered, come back."

"That sounds… Yes."

The Dowager reached into her bodice and pulled out the necklace. Clementha stared at her confused. The eyes widened but the confusion didn't abate when the glow became obvious. After a few seconds, Clementha's eyes narrowed as though she was trying to see past the glow to the pendant beneath.

"This is the real inheritance, Clementha. This is what your mother was afraid of. Still is, I assume, since she's still hiding years after she first learned of it."

Clementha leaned forward, her hand reaching out. It didn't quite bridge the distance and she let the hand fall without having touched the necklace. The look on her face intensified and the Dowager knew that at least, she had Clementha's attention.

"Your family passes this down. Do you remember what they call me?"

Clementha nodded as if in a trance. "The Amaranthine Dowager."

"There's a reason they call me that, truer than they know. How old are you now?"

"Eighteen."

"How old do you think I am?"

Clementha's eyes narrowed as the pieces of the mystery started to resolve themselves. "You look younger than my mother."

"And yet how can that be?" She encouraged Clementha to figure out all of it on her own. There wasn't any fear in the girl's face and already the conversation was going better than the last one she'd had with Clementha's mother.

"Is it the necklace?"

The Dowager shook her head. "Not entirely. Your great-grandfather never wore this necklace. You could not steal this from me and have what I have, if that is what you are asking."

Clementha flushed but nodded, her eyes still stuck on the necklace. It was clear she'd been wondering just that.

"The inheritance cannot be taken by force. It must be given."

"And you want to give it to me?" The tone was reverent and awed as though Clementha wouldn't have expected something so monumental to be hers.

"I'm not willing to go just yet," the Dowager smiled. Clementha's red cheeks reddened further and she waved the words away, stammering. The Dowager held up a hand. "I know you aren't wishing me ill. But I want you to be aware that if you accept, I will become your guardian and you will live here, with me, as I ready you for the other responsibilities. I don't want you living under your father's roof as my heir."

The girl nodded slowly as if she agreed but hadn't expected to be offered such consideration. Again, the Dowager wondered what it would be like to be Albert's daughter.

"Do you have any questions?" the Dowager asked. Excitement thrummed through her veins and she fought to keep it out of her voice and off of her face. She didn't want to alarm the girl.

Clementha's mouth firmed and she nodded. She had many questions and began pelting them at the Dowager. Most of them were about the Amaranth and everything it entailed. She wanted to know how it worked, where the family had gotten it, what it was.

The Dowager answered her questions as best she could until the two of them were worn out. The sun had begun to set and Clementine still waited in the carriage. She had not yet come to check on her daughter's welfare.

"I want you to think about this," the Dowager told Clementha when it was time for her to go. "I will give you two weeks. Don't discuss it with anyone though I know your mother will try. Should you wish to accept and become my heir, I'll expect you in two weeks. If not, I shall see you at the next Christmas party."

They parted quietly, both overflowing with thoughts. Clementha barely remembered to wave from the carriage as the horses sped away. The Dowager thought she caught a glimpse of Clementine's profile inside. She sighed.

The Dowager spent much of the next two weeks waiting at a multitude of windows. She wasn't certain whether or not Clementha would write to say she was coming first. They hadn't discussed that. Her work suffered though her latest assistant was capable enough that the estate didn't suffer.

The problem with waiting on unannounced carriages was that they started to arrive in droves. News of Clementine's visit must have circulated through the relatives for even though they'd all been there for Christmas, little less than half descended. None of the unannounced carriages was the one she was waiting for.

Two weeks came and went. The relatives did more coming than going but provided a frustrating distraction from the fact that Clementha hadn't appeared on their agreed upon date. The family was relieved to realize that there hadn't been a reconciliation between the Dowager and her favorite. This made them more jovial but more irritating.

After the fourth week, relatives stopped coming and started leaving. There was nothing to see but a crotchety old woman who looked older than she ever had. The waiting was taking a toll on the Dowager, for she had not stopped. It had been worse since the deadline for Clementha passed like any other day.

The Dowager hovered around the house like a grey cloud. Her patience was stretched thin and everyone felt it. Though she apologized after every outburst, she could see the servants shooting each other looks. When she yelled at her assistant for making a move with her investments she'd forgotten she'd already agreed to, the Dowager decided it was time to temporarily retire and regain herself.

This meant confinement to her rooms. They were extensive enough that she didn't feel claustrophobic. She ventured out into the gardens, still dusted with snow, but rarely went elsewhere in the house, afraid to encounter someone she might snap at.

Books and food were brought up to her. She spent too much time in her memories and in the past. One day she went through all of her jewelry, trying to recall where she'd gotten it or for which anniversary she'd received it. It was enjoyable but melancholic.

The Dowager wondered if she should remarry and attempt to have a family of her own. The Amaranth might have preserved her enough for that. She entertained this idea for a few days but no longer. The thought of another husband soured her stomach, not to mention the idea of giving birth. She shuddered and retired to bed early.

The next morning, she did not wish to get out of bed. Her most recent book sat on the bed next to her and there was a tray of breakfast on the table. There was no reason to get out of bed at all. She sighed and wondered what would happen to the Amaranth if she died without an heir chosen. Her husband had merely told her not to allow this to happen and had said no more on the subject.

Dozing, the Dowager's reality and dreams began to blend together. The steady beat of her heart thudded in her ears as she lazed about in the bed. When it stopped, she panicked and woke fully.

The knocking started again after a moment and she smiled in relief. A scowl soon followed. She'd left instructions not to be bothered after the breakfast tray.

"Go away."

"Grandmother?"

She sat up at the voice. Clementha. "Clemmy Two?"

"Can I come in?"

"Of course."

In the seconds it took the girl to open the door, the Dowager had fluffed her pillows and fixed her hair. She hoped she didn't look as though she'd been moping or allowing herself to waste away.

The young woman who stood in the doorway smiled widely at the sight of the Dowager. "I heard some of the family's been visiting you."

"I'd been expecting you. Imagine my surprise to see Laticia at the door." The Dowager kept her voice dry. She hoped none of the disappointment bled into her tone.

Clementha's eyebrows puckered as she sat down on the edge of the bed. "I apologize. I should have written. Father had a fall a couple weeks ago. I couldn't tell him I was leaving. He requested I spend the days with him."

"But you're here now."

"He doesn't need me anymore. Mother can tend to him," Clementha said. "I just didn't want to desert him so soon after the fall. I needed to be sure he would recover."

The earnestness in her voice was sweet and the Dowager felt herself relax back against her pillows. She reached out for the hand that sat on her coverlet.

"I'm glad to see you, Clemmy Two."

Clementha grinned and blushed at the name, raising her eyes to meet the Dowager's.

"Do you want it?" the Dowager asked, her voice intense.

It took the girl a moment to answer, which the Dowager approved of even as it made her nervous.

But Clementha nodded. "I'm not afraid."

"Good. You shouldn't be. Be wary and careful but never be afraid. It can be an amazing gift."

Clementha's eyes shone as she nodded again. "I have so many things I want to do. So many ideas."

The Dowager smiled indulgently. She'd never felt that, the inheritance overshadowed by the death of her husband.

"But you must promise me you will do something with it," she told the young woman, her hand tightening on the smaller one. "Do something with it. Make it worthwhile."

"What did you do with it?"

"Not enough." She'd lived more than her one lifetime. That was it. But even if that was all Clemmy Two did, the Dowager wouldn't be unhappy. Life was for the young.

"It won't be a waste, Grandmother. We'll do such things together, you and I."

The Dowager grinned, feeling some of the girl's infectious life seep into her cold hand. Maybe this new companion would make her final years as sweet as her husband had made her initial ones. And when it was time to go, she could do so gladly, knowing that she'd given a gift to someone who would use it.

THE INHERITANCE

He watched Althea from the bed. She'd slung a silk dressing gown over her shoulders before sitting at her vanity, gazing down at her jewelry.

"You shouldn't worry," he told her, smiling fondly.

She shot him a sharp glance through the looking glass, making his smile widen.

"You know I must," she replied.

Her long fingers stirred the pieces of jewelry she'd amassed over the length of their marriage.

"It won't change anything," he said.

"It might."

His family was coming to celebrate his birthday and neither of them was happy about it. He could handle small doses of his children. Althea, his fourth wife, preferred not to see them. He understood her feelings all too well. She was greatly resented for diminishing the inheritance.

"Why not wear the locket from your mother?" he asked. It was an unassuming piece.

Althea wrinkled her nose at it. "I don't like it."

"You never wear it."

"Because I don't like it."

He subsided with a laugh.

It was his last laugh of the week. Though his children and grandchildren didn't know his exact age, they knew he was old enough to have declared an heir. That he hadn't yet made them anxious.

When his children weren't vying for his attention, the smarter ones turned their eye towards his wife. Normally she was an outsider at these functions, only beset by the grandchildren too young to know better and Florence, his youngest. She'd looked up to Althea as a mother since hers had died.

"Althea?"

She was alone and sat enthroned on a tall red chair, watching everyone impassively. It was that expression on her face that had called him over. It never meant anything good.

"Laurinia wants to know what I'll do when you're gone," Althea replied. "Since she won't let me stay in the manor."

His hand tightened on the back of the chair where it had been resting lightly. "She's always been spiteful," he replied, his voice low.

Althea gave him a small smile. It was a public smile and he wished for the celebrations to be over. She was the last wife he would ever have and they enjoyed each other thoroughly, much more so when they were alone. It hurt him to see his children hurt her.

"I'm looking forward to that spite when I'm alone," Althea said.

"You won't be at her mercy," he told her.

It was the first time he'd even obliquely mentioned his plans for an heir. Everyone, including Laurinia, believed his eldest would take the inheritance. They also all expected to receive something. It would be a joy to disillusion a few of them. Those he actually favored, he'd already made provisions for by setting them up nicely either with good spouses or with good work.

"It becomes more and more depressing, does it not?" she asked him rhetorically.

He gazed around the extended receiving room at the crowds of his offspring. There was something newly depressing about it, especially when he glanced down at his wife again. She was getting older in a way that he wasn't. Turning thirty-six this year, he could already see her slowing down. It was almost imperceptible but he'd been through three wives by now.

He watched Althea from the bed. She sat at her vanity, looking through her jewelry but without the tension in her shoulders. She was humming.

"I'm getting old," he told her, fingering the ring on his index finger. Its ethereal glow lit the bedclothes blue.

"You don't look old," she told him with a grin over her shoulder.

"But I'm old," he argued. "I'm getting tired."

Something in his tone must have alarmed her. She spun, dislodging her dressing gown and flashing her bare shoulder.

"Tired?"

He nodded. "I'm tired of watching my wives fade and my children become greedier and malicious. It's tiring."

Althea sat on the bed next to him, reaching out to grab the hand with the ring. She turned it into the morning sunshine where it sparkled.

"Nothing's wrong, is it?" she asked, tapping the ring.

He shook his head. "Nothing's wrong. And you're right, I don't look old. But Ally, I *feel* old."

Leaning over, she touched their foreheads, threading one hand through his full head of hair. "Maybe you need some time away. Would you like to visit the coast?"

He shook his head, reaching up to capture her hand. "I'm tired, Ally."

She drew back, frowning at him. "What are you saying?"

"I don't want to see you get older than me and then die. You've never had anything but me."

"I've never wanted anything but you. And I did have sixteen years," she told him with a grin. "They weren't anything special."

"I'm going to choose an heir," he said, cutting through her attempts at humor.

Her skin tightened and that impassive expression returned. He could see her flicking through the eight children and countless grandchildren, trying to choose who he would name.

"I want you to take it," he told her.

Distressed, she stared down at him, her eyes only briefly flickering to the ring on his hand.

"Who else can I trust with the Amaranth?" he asked her.

"But I can't be your heir," she said, her eyes still wide.

"Yes, you can. I trust you with it."

He removed the ring, pressing it into her palm. It dropped from her hand once he'd withdrawn his own.

"Althea…"

"I don't want it! Put it back on. We've only had twenty years and you promised me a lifetime." There were tears in her eyes. The ring lay on the bed between them. "How can you expect me to live forever without you?"

"It won't be forever. Someday you'll be tired. But Ally, I don't want another birthday."

It was with trembling hands that Althea picked up the ring and slid it on her finger. The blue glowed even more brightly under the fall of her tears.

Lost and Found

They'd been playing hide and seek when *he* found her. Sven heard his sister scream from his bedroom. It was nighttime and he always hid in his bedroom at night when they played.

Their father hadn't been playing. He wasn't even supposed to be home. Trembling, Sven cowered under his bed. The shouts were punctuated by slaps. It was going to be a bad night.

He didn't know why she was being beaten. It didn't really matter. He was the only one safe in the house, being the son, the heir. Too cowardly to try and interfere, he huddled under the bed, hoping it would be over soon.

She'd been seeking on the floor below him, underneath his bedroom. Sven could hear everything too easily. He flinched with every blow but even when the inevitable quiet fell, Sven couldn't move.

He could hear his father's footsteps as they climbed the stairs. They paused outside his door. Sven held his breath, afraid for his father to hear even a soft inhale. After a heart-stopping minute, the footsteps moved on. Still, Sven held his breath until he heard his father's door slam.

He found his sister propped up in the threshold of the sitting room, half sprawled into the corridor. She was leaning against the doorjamb as if it was the only thing holding her up. It probably was.

"I found you," she whispered, smiling at him blearily. One eye was swelling shut.

He stared at her. Filtered moonlight skewered her familiar features, making her look demonic. But Sven wasn't afraid. He'd seen her like this before. Often.

His sister sighed, gingerly leaning her head back against the doorjamb. Her arms and legs were splayed out across the wooden floors.

"Mother went to get the journal," she told him.

It was his cue to leave. The mention of the journal was enough to make him shudder. Though his mother promised him it was only leather and nothing more repugnant, Sven couldn't believe it. But he hadn't heard or seen their mother and he didn't want to leave his sister there alone.

"Sven."

Their mother's soft tread barely disturbed the silence. She stopped a distance from the two of them. Sven could see the journal clutched in her hands.

He stiffened, trying not to look at the leather-bound book. The darkness was thickest around the journal, the silence starker.

"I'll come say goodnight in a bit," his mother said.

Sven took it as the dismissal it was and fled. He'd never seen what the journal was capable of. He'd only seen it come out when his sister needed it.

He woke the next morning to more shouting. This time, cowering in his bed did nothing to stop it from coming into his room.

The door burst open and his father filled the doorway, glowering at him hatefully, eyes filled with suspicion. It was the first time Sven's father had ever looked at him like that. Sven's skin crawled in premonition.

"Where is she? Where is your sister?"

Terrified, Sven couldn't answer.

"I know she told you where she was going!" His father slapped Sven's face hard, snapping Sven's head to the side.

It was the first time Sven had ever been hit.

When Sven didn't answer, his father pulled him up by the front of his nightgown and smacked him again, this time harder. He threw Sven to the bed and Sven's head cracked on the iron frame.

He groaned, unable to help himself. His head lolled on his pillow, a lump forming. His eyesight blurred but he could make out a scrawl on his forearm.

You're it

Sven cowered in the alleyway, peering out around the corner as best he could without being seen. In one hand he clutched a crumpled, stained piece of paper, in the other hand, he held a bag.

The house was just across the street from where he stood. It had taken weeks to find it as the last address he'd been given turned out to be wrong. Sven shivered, wriggling his toes in the hope that the feeling might return to them.

He was afraid to venture towards the house, in case it was the wrong one. He wasn't sure he could survive another disappointment. There was no plan after this one.

A carriage pulled up to the house. Sven stiffened, ducking back inside the alley as a figure emerged from the house. He couldn't make out if it was a man or a woman as it was quickly shielded by the carriage.

His grip on the paper tightened and it crinkled in response. As the carriage sped away, Sven steeled his resolve and hurried out of the alley. When he made it to the house, he ducked around the back, where there would be a separate entrance. He wasn't good enough for the front door of this house.

No one answered. Sven reached into his bag, groping. When he touched the journal, he recoiled at first before clutching at it. His fear spurred him on.

Sven nudged at the door and it opened. He stepped inside, listening intently for any signs of life. There were none that he could hear.

He made his way through the kitchen, into the house proper. There were no servants. The floorboards creaked under his feet and he froze.

"Richard?" a voice croaked.

Sven's heart thundered and his palms sweated. He stood there in the middle of the corridor, wondering what to do next.

"Richard, is that you?"

It was her. Sven felt his eyes water at the voice he hadn't heard in years. She groaned and he followed the sounds until he saw her.

She was sprawled against a couch, wheezing. She looked as though she'd been in a fight. Lifting her head, she had to squint to make him out. When she didn't recognize him as Richard, she stirred anxiously.

"Who-?"

Sven stood on the threshold, trying to smile as his sister stared at him.

"Found you," Sven whispered.

The Poisoned Perfume

Malena scanned the temporary stables laid out in the expansive courtyard. Though she was supposed to be there for a set of carriage horses, that wasn't the flesh she was looking at. She allowed a fan to flutter in front of her face, distracting viewers from the sharp dart of her glance.

Ostlers, horse trainers and stablemen were the usual fellows at these events but because there was also a display of the newest fashion in carriages, there was also a higher station of people threaded through. Malena knew that before she'd arrived, five hours after the event started. It was the reason she was there. A meat market of a different sort.

It was the perfect avenue to insert herself into Capeland's society. Purchasing her extravagant townhome in the center of the city had helped but she needed something else. She needed people to see her, to wonder and eventually, to invite her to their gatherings. Husbands, nowadays, weren't as simply come by.

There weren't many other women around, certainly not ones dressed as Malena was dressed. She intended to catch someone's eye that day, even if nothing came of it. She strolled leisurely over the grey cobbles, past the horses, her manservant following a few steps behind as he always did.

Malena stopped in front of the new carriages. It was the expected destination for a woman of her station. She surely couldn't be looking at the horses and Malena mentally scoffed, flicking her fan up again so that she could eye the men around her.

Almost every one was sending her sideways looks, trying to be discrete about their interest. She smiled from behind the fan, pleased. But as minutes passed and no one made to approach her, the smile began to fall. There was something wrong.

She circled one carriage and then the other, being watched by the men selling them. Catching her reflection in a wide metal fitting, Malena frowned. Was she looking that old again? She turned her head from side to side, scowling at the wrinkles she could see. It took her a minute to realize that the scowl wasn't helping.

"Is everything alright with the carriage, ma'am?" a male voice jostled her out of her thoughts.

She turned at the plebian tone, her scowl still partially in place. He stood to the side of the carriage, a proprietary hand on it, a worried look on his face.

"There's nothing wrong with it that I can see," she told him. A well-shined shoe caught her eye and she let her gaze run the length of the man. A little too young for her.

"You were frowning dreadfully at it."

Surprised that he was still speaking to her, and so familiarly, Malena turned back to stare at the young man. Relief lit his face and he was grinning at her. She let her surprise show in her expression. Slowly he realized himself and his face turned a most intriguing color.

"Pardon me, ma'am," he mumbled, backing away from her, almost tripping in his mortification.

Her interest piqued, she followed him around the carriage. He didn't know what to do with himself or her and they did a full circle before he stopped backing away. Pulling himself together, he straightened his shirt and tried to smile. It wavered.

"Are you interested in one of our carriages, ma'am? Perhaps to carry you and your family?"

She smiled at him, with more than a hint of teeth. "Oh, not anymore."

He stuttered in response, not sure what she meant. Her grin widened in reply and the blush was back on his face.

"Did I say something to dissuade you?" he asked, concerned and maybe a little frightened.

"No. I wasn't here for the carriages. It's just little old me in my house and I wanted some fresh air." She stepped towards him predatorily, forgetting about the real reason she'd come to this little event.

Malena saw the run of his Adam's apple. How delicious. She let her eyes wander up and down the specimen in front of her. He looked better and better and his frightened naiveté made him even more attractive. The men she married tended to be boors, jaded by their lives of wealth and leisure. This one shone in comparison.

It had been some time since she'd allowed herself some fun. Though she'd taken a small break after the death of her last husband, she'd really only been settling affairs and choosing a new city. Her life was often overrun by logistics.

"I wouldn't mark you as old," he stammered, turning even redder with his clumsy attempt at flattery.

Malena smiled and coquetted as though his flattery had succeeded. She knew she didn't look *old*. She would never allow such a thing to happen. Her lifestyle depended too much on looking young.

His response was interesting. Her behavior must have given him some small measure of confidence because he straightened and tried again.

"And if you don't have a husband, then it must be by your choice. Who could resist you?" It was a much better attempt and the fact that he'd tried at all, in the face of his almost crippling embarrassment earlier only drew her in more.

"Orval!"

At the sound of what had to be his name, the young man leapt and whirled. A much larger man stood behind him, a glower hiding under a mammoth mustache, his eyes almost shadowed entirely by his eyebrows.

"Ye-yes, Mr. Helmer?"

"Are you bothering this young woman?" It wasn't much of a question. It was clear from the look on his face that he was certain of the situation.

While Orval stood, stammering and flickering bewildered, frightened looks between Malena and Mr. Helmer, the older man decided to ignore him entirely.

"I'm so sorry for Orval's behavior. He isn't fit for polite company," Mr. Helmer said, his obsequiousness irritating Malena.

"I've not been damaged by it," Malena said, trying to hide her frustration at being interrupted. "But I don't think I'll look at the carriages any further."

Her fun spoiled, and her mood as well, Malena turned and headed for the entrance of the courtyard. When she was far enough away and could no longer feel their glances on her back, she beckoned to her manservant. He scurried to her side, pacing her. She resisted reaching out to him while they were still in the public eye.

"I want you to invite the young man to the house. Discretely."

Her manservant nodded.

Malena returned to the new townhouse and waited. She tried not to think of it as waiting, but that was the reality. She'd changed from her earlier outfit into something more comfortable and slightly more provocative. Hoping that the look on Orval's face would be everything she imagined, she lounged in her formal sitting room, trying not to watch out the front window.

Her manservant returned with Orval in tow.

Malena paused a moment before rising when Orval was introduced at the threshold of the sitting room. She wanted him to have the full effect. His gulp was visible across the room and Malena waved the manservant away.

"I-I'm sorry for my inappropriateness earlier," Orval tried to apologize.

Smiling, Malena was delighted that he thought she'd invited him for an apology. His eyes widened as she approached, still not having replied. She could see him trying to keep his eyes on her face. Even his ears were red.

"I hope you didn't get into too much trouble with Mr. Helmer," she said, her voice low and intimate.

It took Orval a moment to reply. The bewildered expression still hadn't cleared as she reached out to touch his arm. He had no idea what was happening.

"He's my uncle so he can't let me go," Orval eventually said.

Malena nodded as though this was excellent news. "I am so pleased to hear it. I would be devastated if I had been the cause of something so catastrophic."

His eyebrows dipped as he tried to understand what she was saying. Malena couldn't be sure if he was too distracted by the warm presence of her hand on his arm or if he couldn't puzzle out the words she was using. Either was acceptable to her.

It had been far too long since she'd had an innocent to despoil. Her hand crept up his arm while he stuttered. It must have been a habit of his. She wondered if she could break him of it.

But instead of eventually coming up with an answer to her comment, what he managed was, "What are you doing?"

Her grin sharpened. "What do you think I'm doing?"

Malena's hand had crept up to wrap around the back of his neck. Her fingers swirled the soft hairs they found there. Orval stood stock-still, letting her do as she wished. The skin on the back of his neck was hot to her touch.

"Do you wish to talk more of Mr. Helmer?" Malena whispered in his ear, leaning close so that he could smell her perfume. She'd dotted on more of her disappearing vintage just for him.

Orval shook his head frantically, then more carefully as if not to dislodge her hand. She tightened her grip and pulled his head down towards hers.

"Then I don't wish to talk anymore at all," she said, letting the idea ghost over him.

Orval shuddered but didn't resist when her grip moved to his hand and she began tugging him out of the formal sitting room. His feet stumbled on the stairs heading upwards but his gaze was fogged, his mouth almost slack.

"Do you know where we are going, Orval?" Malena asked.

He shook his head as they paused on the landing. She arched an eyebrow at him. He flushed and then nodded slowly. She grinned at him and resumed climbing. He still didn't even know her name.

Malena gazed down at the invitation one more time. Her full name was written out beautifully and she stroked the paper with soft fingertips. The invitation was the result of one of her forays into

Capeland. The horse hunting hadn't gone as well as she'd hoped, though she'd had some amusement out of it all the same.

But its lack of success had only spurred her to try harder at her next gambol. There hadn't been any deep connections or men she'd felt sure of but she'd obviously made an impression on somebody. The result was sitting in front of her now.

"I don't like that dress," a petulant voice came from the curtained bed behind her.

Malena grinned at her reflection briefly. "Orval, you are so delightfully transparent." A sigh was heaved in her direction. "Now stop sulking and come fasten this for me."

She held out the jet necklace she'd be wearing. The perfume bottle that she always wore was still on a thin chain around her neck, tucked into her cleavage. Another sigh and then the rustling of bedclothes. Orval appeared moments later, shirtless.

Malena's expression was bland as she held the necklace out closer to him. He took it with his third sigh of the day.

"Orval."

At the sound of his name, he straightened and bent to ease the necklace over her head. The jet beads slid across her skin like ice. She shivered at the delicious sensation. Orval's fingers followed with a conflicting warmth.

"Do you have to go?" he asked with a precious hesitancy. The petulance was gone.

Despite his weeks in her bed, he wasn't entirely confident of his place, which was just as she wanted it. Against his prior announcement and belief, Mr. Helmer could and did dismiss him from employment. While initially Malena had felt triumphant over the news, Orval's following depression over his impending poverty became tiresome. She rejected the twinge of guilt over his dismissal and hired him temporarily though she had no need of another servant or footsman.

"Of course I'm going," Malena told him impatiently. "A husband won't just come to me." Not any longer. Now she had to go hunting.

It wasn't the first time she'd mentioned husbands to Orval, though it was the first time she'd mentioned them with any seriousness. Orval's face tightened and his hands fell from her collarbones.

Malena watched him closely as he shuffled towards his pile of clothes. He knew he wouldn't be spending the night now. Though he was naïve, he was not stupid.

"Gerald will feed you before you go," she told him, turning her gaze back to her reflection. "And they'll need your help with the carriage."

The continual teetering between personal and impersonal interactions had Orval off-kilter. Malena smiled at him before he left, making him pause momentarily on the threshold.

Her manservant helped her finish dressing. Malena employed no women after catching her first husband with a succession of the female household servants. And after Sven had found her, she'd never needed a personal servant again. He was everything she could ever want or need.

She dressed mostly in black with hints of color to lighten the austerity. Malena would judge the effect from Orval's face. He waited at the bottom of the steps to help her out the front door and into the waiting carriage.

Pausing on the landing, making sure Orval looked up, Malena waited a brief moment. His face slackened and she could see his Adam's apple bob from there. It brought back memories of the first day they met and she smiled.

After that, his face shifted, freezing between awe and upset. Malena could just about read his thought process on his face. He wasn't sure he was entitled to feel jealousy but it was impossible to suppress.

Malena swept past him as he scrambled to open the front door for her. He followed her down the front steps and into the street. She waited on the sidewalk for him to pull down the little carriage steps. When his hand was outstretched to help, she took it, sliding into the small space.

The road was bumpy on the way to the ball. Malena didn't mind, fanning herself in the warm spring air, watching the houses pass by out the window. It wasn't the first ball she'd attended alone but she had the momentary thought that it would have been a pleasure to take Orval with her. As soon as the thought appeared, she brushed it away, scoffing at herself.

The rest of the trip was spent picking out the attributes she wanted in this next husband. She wanted a younger one, if it could be helped, with significantly more funds than the last one. Malena was also hoping for one she wouldn't mind living with, though she knew that would be a difficult requirement to fill. She hadn't seen anything in Capeland's society that would lead her to believe the men were different here to anywhere else.

Maybe she would be able to find a shy, naïve one, similar to Orval. That would be a delight, though they were few in numbers and often they did not attend such functions as the one she was driving towards. Wrapped up in her thoughts of her future spouse, Malena missed it when they arrived.

She startled when the door popped open beside her. Scolding herself and settling her heart, she set a serene expression on her face and took the hand presented to her. Nodding at her coachman, Malena swept through the gates and up the stairs towards the ball.

Holding out her invitation, Malena barely paused at the entrance. She gave her name to be announced and then waited at the smaller double doors to be declared into the party. When her name was called, Malena strolled in, keeping her footsteps small and neat. She didn't look in either direction though she noted who stopped to give her a second glance.

It was busier than she'd expected with a wealth of younger people in attendance. She allowed herself a small smile as she began to circulate the room. It took four passes for her to pick out the six different men she would angle to meet. On the fifth pass, she had to remove two. One, for seeming to have a female escort and the second, for having been permanently attached to his mother on all five of her circuits.

That left four. Malena preferred conversation to dancing and she took a glass of wine off of a tray and slowly headed towards her first prey. He was taller than her by a good amount, with dark, thick hair. His eyes were too large for her tastes but his shoes were well-made and he filled out the shoulders of his jacket nicely.

Drink in hand, Malena circled closer and closer to the target. She stood in front of him, off to the side, facing the dancers. Swaying in time with the music, Malena took a deep drink of her wine, rolling the liquid over her tongue. One of the men she'd been watching joined the dancers at the next song and she narrowed her eyes, trying to decipher if he was actually with someone.

"Excuse me," her prey said from behind her.

Malena turned slightly, pretending to be surprised. "Yes?"

"I feel certain that I've been to so many of these parties that I would recognize everyone of note," he said, smiling, "but I don't remember your face."

Malena smiled back at him, taking another sip of her wine while she made him wait for a response. "You wouldn't have seen my face before."

His eyebrows lifted in mock surprise. "Indeed. Would you care to join the dancers while you tell me more about yourself and what you're doing in Capeland?"

Malena did not want to join the dancers but couldn't think of a polite, intriguing way of refusing. Instead, she nodded and left her glass on a circulating tray. The man lifted his arm in expectation and she lightly let her hand fall on top of it.

They swept out onto the ballroom floor when the music ended for a moment, signaling a new dance. Malena was a graceful dancer from endless tutors as a child. It had been one of her punishments. Now, she danced only when she wished to impress. It was a means to an end, never something enjoyable.

The dance was too rigorous for much talk and they only skimmed the basics of each other's lives and personalities. Malena knew it would be so as soon as she heard the music. Her partner didn't appear to mind and his face was flushed with the thrill of the dance. It made him all the more attractive and Malena decided she could perhaps overlook the largeness of his eyes. She wanted to laugh at her pettiness but tucked it away behind her carefully crafted expression.

Soon, though not soon enough, the dance ended and they retired to the sidelines. His eyes glittered as he looked at her and Malena reached for another glass of wine, feeling pleased with her success. She might not even need to remember the other three faces she'd picked out.

"You are a marvelous dancer," he told her. "I thought you might be, seeing your grace off of the dance floor."

Malena smiled up at him demurely. "You're too kind."

"Not at all. Would you like another turn on the floor?"

Surprised, it took Malena a moment to demur. Surely the once was enough to capture his interest? But as soon as she said no, he began to get restless, his attention wandering. Quickly, within minutes, he'd made a pathetic excuse and left her alone on the edge of the dance floor.

Bewildered, Malena stared after him. It was the first time in a long time she'd been left like that. It took her far longer than it should have to shake the humiliation of it off. Scowling, she turned to find one of the other men she'd picked out.

The second man was already watching her from closer to the door. Malena smiled coquettishly at him, wondering if he was actually watching her or if he was staring at someone else. The young man raised his glass in her direction, answering her question. Malena held his eye, determined not to give in after her last humiliation.

When she didn't move, he began to weave his way through the brightly colored people, almost in time to the music. Malena watched him carefully. He seemed courteous as he moved through the crowds, trying not to bump anyone and apologizing when he did. That was promising, if he should prove to be a soft touch. She'd never yet managed a husband with that trait.

He reached her side, looking slightly winded. Smiling uncertainly, he introduced himself as Harold. Malena gave him her first name only, wondering if Harold was wealthy. Not everyone in the room would be. The higher echelons were masters of hidden secrets. It would be a pity to dismiss this one over money. His blond hair appealed to her though usually she preferred brunettes.

"I saw you dancing earlier," Harold told her, nodding at the dance floor.

"Yes, the man who asked was quite insistent," she replied.

"You were beautiful."

Malena's smile widened. While flattery wouldn't move her from her goals, it was still always welcome when it was sincerely meant.

"Thank you," she said.

"But I was wondering," he said, pausing before continuing. "I noticed that you're wearing unrelieved black." There was a brief pause once again while Malena waited. When she showed no inclination of speaking, he asked, with a grimace, much more straightforwardly, "Are you in mourning?"

It was a rather personal question to ask to a stranger and Malena gave him a look that let him know that. He flushed but still looked as though he expected an answer.

"I'm not in mourning," she said. He relaxed, making her realize that she hadn't noticed he'd been tense. "Though I did lose a husband a year ago."

The tension was back and the hand that held a glass of wine shook. "Only a year ago? My deepest condolences."

"Thank you, Harold. We weren't married very long but it was still a surprise," she said, trying to look wistful with only a tint of sadness.

"It's such a pity to be widowed at your age," he agreed. "I hope he left you comfortable in your grief."

Was he angling for the state of her finances? Malena tried to discern his intentions from his face. Something had made him uncomfortable again, that was certain.

As if realizing that his statement could be misconstrued, he started stammering an apology which got interrupted by an explanation. It went on and on while Malena watched in amused horror. There was no escaping this. Until he surprised her once more by retreating.

"I hope for an end to your grief and your mourning," he said stiffly, bowing formally before rushing away.

Again, Malena was left staring after a man she'd been targeting, wondering what had happened. This time, she finished her wine, letting the cool liquid attempt to soothe her sore ego. She tugged on the thin chain around her neck, pulling the pendant free. Her fingers wandered over the familiar whorls of the glass. The motion, ingrained after years of wearing the necklace, calmed her.

Before she went back to her hunt, Malena took some time to collect herself. She'd been at this too long to be confounded twice like an amateur. There had to be something else at play. As she walked another circuit of the room, she unlatched the perfume bottle nestled in her cleavage and dabbed some on her neck. The bottle was almost empty, worrying her. She needed a husband and soon.

The pungent smell attacked her nose before dissipating into the air around her. The smell helped focus her. She couldn't locate one of the two remaining men so when she spotted one of them, she immediately headed in his direction. This one was, perhaps, the least attractive of the specimens she'd chosen.

As she neared him, like the last man, he was watching her, this time, with open appraisal. She raised an eyebrow at that and he grinned. They met halfway, close to the walls, as far from the dance floor as they could be.

"Let me guess," he asked before an introduction. "Husband-hunting?"

Both shocked at his audacity and intrigued, Malena nodded. "Of course, isn't everyone else here? This is one extended courtship ritual, is it not?"

He laughed at that. "Malcom," he told her.

"Malena Torrence."

"I'll be forthright, Malena Torrence. You're older than I'm looking for, however, I have an uncle who would find you delightful. He's well off and hosting a dinner in a week. I can extend an invitation if you'd like to meet him."

Malena was still reeling from the age comment and couldn't immediately pull together an answer. This was the oldest of the men she'd been looking at and he was older than she looked by quite a ways.

"I see I've surprised you and perhaps not pleasantly," he observed. "I don't intend to be hurtful, merely observing."

Stiffly nodding at him, she tried to keep her expression blank. Underneath, her mind was still reeling. Had she noticed any excess aging in the mirror as she was getting ready? Perhaps Orval had distracted her from seeing what was really there.

"Would you like an invitation?" Malcom asked, cutting through the whirling thoughts.

"Certainly," Malena croaked out. "It's always good to meet new people."

She managed a smile and Malcom laughed, sounding pleased with himself.

"Yes, I think my uncle will greatly enjoy you." He took her address and promised to send her an invitation. Quickly afterwards, Malcom made his farewells and bowed out of her presence.

Malena watched him go. She left not much longer after, afraid to stay in the brightly lit room with the beautiful, smiling people dancing and chatting gaily. Feeling like a seething mass of black emotions, Malena climbed into her carriage much earlier than she intended. The bumpy ride home did little or nothing to soothe her.

Over and over her fingers rubbed familiar paths over the tiny perfume bottle she wore around her neck in a dated fashion. Leaning her head against the window of the carriage, she tried to catch a good look at her faint reflection. Lines she hadn't seen before covered her face and her fingers investigated them, smoothing them out.

She stepped out of the carriage when it stopped, tightly gripping the driver's hand. Almost reluctant to let go, Malena finally managed to free him once she was on the sidewalk, staring up at her house. It was dark and looked empty. Orval wouldn't be waiting for her and going inside to bed alone wasn't something she wanted to do.

The carriage drove off behind her and Malena stood there for a bit longer before deciding on a walk. She had problems to think through. The house was central and lamps lit the paths her feet tread. Malena didn't know her new city very well so she stayed on the same road, pacing long stretches at a time.

Very few people were out on the streets with her. She kept her shawl wrapped tightly about her, one hand on her necklace. Her thoughts wouldn't settle and she couldn't work through anything. Instead, she relived the humiliating events of the ball over and over. Her worries circled around behind them.

She was so tied up in her thoughts that she never heard the fast clip of the shoes behind her. It wasn't the noise at all that Malena noticed. It was the sudden and tight grip on her arm.

Malena tried to yank free and turn at the same time. Only the second motion was mildly successful. The man's face was hidden in the flare of light behind him and she opened her mouth to shout when he clapped a fat hand over her face, pulling her away from the lights of the street and into one of the side alleys.

Wriggling and kicking out at him, Malena managed to sink her teeth into the thick pad of his hand. He howled and cried out an oath but his grip never wavered. He only had one of her arms and Malena reached up for her necklace, jerking the perfume bottle from its lid.

With a heave, Malena twisted in his grip and threw the perfume in his eyes. This time when he cried out, he let go of her, hunching over his burning face. Malena kicked him in the groin with her pointed shoe and he collapsed, bellowing.

Before he had a chance to recover, Malena grabbed a broken piece of brick she'd stumbled over and turning, brought it down on the side of his face. It sunk into his cheek, shattering some of his teeth. His hand shot out, clutching at her ankle through her dress. Panting, Malena tried to balance, kicking at him.

Her boot struck his stomach and she almost toppled. He pulled on her leg even as he whined in pain. Afraid of what would happen if she went down, Malena pounded at his head again, catching the back of his skull. This time, she heard the crack she'd been looking for and his hand fell from her leg, limp.

Once he was still, with trembling hands, Malena dropped the brick. Scrounging about in the dirt of the alley, she located the lid to her perfume bottle. She reattached it and straightened up, dry sobs wracking her frame.

Afraid, Malena could feel herself shuddering in the aftermaths of adrenaline. She stared down at her attacker, his hands fallen from his face. The damage done by the perfume was immediate and sickening. The perfume had eaten away at his eyes and was still working on the flesh of his face.

What she could see of him wasn't familiar. Malena straightened, feeling faint. She stepped over his body and stumbled out of the alleyway, into the street.

There was no one there. Malena headed down the street, towards her house. The closer she got, the quicker she started moving until she was running down the street and up her front stairs. Once she was inside, she collapsed on the entryway rug.

Cursing and crying, Malena wiped at her face with the back of one hand, and then the other.

"Sven!" Malena shouted, her voice garbled. "Sven!"

Her free hand grasped her perfume bottle. She'd used it all. Every bit that was remaining was gone.

Sven clattered down the back stairs. She could hear him hurrying and she swallowed the next shout deep in her throat where it unexpectedly turned into a sob. Her manservant rounded the corner, his face going slack with horror when he caught sight of her.

Malena tried to laugh at the expression. Surely he'd seen her worse. She knew for a fact that he'd seen her look worse. Sven fell at her feet, his hands reaching out towards her, stopping just shy of touching her. He didn't know what to do.

"Sven, I need you to do something for me," she said. The words wavered and she took a few deep breaths, trying to settle herself. She couldn't leave that man out there. What if he'd been sent for her?

"Malena," he said, his eyes wide.

"There's a man in an alleyway. I want you to fetch him." Then she told him where he would find the man and asked him to take the carriage. Sven wouldn't manage the big man by himself. Orval popped into her mind before she rudely dismissed him.

Sven went out the back way. Malena was still leaning against the front door and couldn't be budged. Her body felt thick, heavy like the despondency that settled over her. Tears still ran over her face, down her throat and eventually settled into the fabric of her dress.

As she sat there, she wondered at the emotions of it all. She'd barely been hurt. Her childhood had comprised more nasty shocks and pains than a failed attack on the street. She had scars bigger than the bruises his hands would leave. It was the surprise of it, the fear. The horrible worry that maybe she'd been found, that Sven had been found. Everything seemed to be going wrong.

When she heard Sven return, his familiar noises at the back of the house, she decided she had to fix it. First, she would find out what the man knew, if he knew anything at all. There was every chance it had been an opportunist's attack and nothing more. For all she knew, no one was hunting for her.

But no matter what, everything would start going right again. First she would take care of her perfume bottle. She couldn't leave it empty. Not after that night at the ball. She was clearly starting to look too old. And at the same time, she could take care of another problem.

"To the cellar?" Sven asked, appearing in the hallway, sweating.

"Yes, Sven. To the cellar."

She waited until she heard the thump of the body as it rolled down the stairs to her workroom beneath the house. Once she'd heard it, Malena climbed to her feet. She wiped her face one last time and straightened her dress. There was a lot of work to be done and this time, she was looking forward to it. It would be a release for the emotions she felt too small to contain.

Malena stood at the top of the cellar stairs. Sven had lit the cellar and now stood behind her, offering her a gas lamp.

"Is he awake?" Malena asked.

"Yes."

As he responded, Malena could hear whimpers from downstairs.

"Good. You can go back to bed. Thank you, Sven, for your help."

Sven's face glowed with a surprised pleasure and Malena twisted to lean back and cup his face, pressing a soft kiss on his lips. She watched him leave, smiling. Then, she turned back to the stairs.

"Are you ready for me?" she asked as she began her descent.

When Malena climbed the stairs back up into the daylight, she was filthy and exhausted but her perfume bottle sloshed in her grip. Dawn had come and gone and Malena was left wondering what time it was. It didn't matter.

Her manservant knew not to bother her after a night in the cellar. Malena needed to be alone and so she climbed her stairs up to her bedroom in a completely silent house. The looking glass beckoned to her and against her will, she sat at her vanity.

The reflection staring back at her was empty-eyed and smeared with unmentionable stains. But leaning forward, Malena frowned at it for other reasons. Now that she was looking she could see why the men at the ball had shown little personal interest in her. Wrinkles she didn't remember seeing had cropped up. Her skin was starting to sag with age.

Her hands shook as she uncorked her perfume bottle from her neck. Too much of it sloshed over the lip as she dabbed it on her neck. The smell wasn't overly pleasant but she ignored it, leaning even closer to the mirror.

The skin tightened minutely as she watched. Some of the larger wrinkles shrunk. Pulling away from the looking glass, she examined herself at a length. A few of the years had dropped from her face. Not quite enough though. She frowned again. It wasn't the best perfume she'd made and she sighed.

There was nothing to be done for it at the moment. Malena retired to her bathing room. It was a luxury she simply had to have for instances such as this. There was no removing the stench of her work in a wash basin with lukewarm water.

Malena lounged in the large tub made for two. Luxuriating in the scalding water, she tried to forget the events of the night. It was more difficult than it should have been. When forgetting refused to work, Malena instead turned her thoughts to analyzing.

What was it about the night that wouldn't release its grip on her? The shock of being attacked when she thought she was safe? That was certainly a large aspect of it. If she hadn't had as much perfume or hadn't been able to grab the bottle, the night could have ended very differently. Maybe it was the fear. She'd promised herself that she would never allow herself to be beaten again.

While she was working in her cellar, Malena had taken the opportunity to speak to her attacker. It gave him a chance to relax, to believe that nothing she could do would harm him. It was a mistaken belief but Malena found it made things easier for them both, for a while.

He hadn't known her as she'd feared he had. He hadn't been sent for her and there was no one else coming. There was no agenda behind his attack aside from the mundane. He'd merely chosen the wrong victim. She'd looked easy.

Running her fingers down her legs, Malena stared at the back of her hands. They were still pale and smooth, though she fancied she could see impending age on them.

The perfume wasn't doing the good it should have been. The man wasn't pure enough. Malena ducked under the water. The heat burned at her face, prickling her nerves. It had been a long time since she'd been foiled in her plans. She was used to getting her way now. Perhaps she'd gone soft.

There was a persistent knocking on the bathing room door. Malena scowled at it. She recognized it as her manservant's knock. Orval's was quite different.

"Can it wait, Sven?" she called, irritated at being interrupted.

"Notes of promise to be paid, Malena," he said through the door, keeping his voice as hushed as possible as though it might be overheard.

Malena's frown deepened. "Bring them in."

Wiping her hands on one of the fluffy towels waiting beside the tub on a green chair, Malena sat up. Sven swung the door open, shuffling in, envelopes in his hand. Irritated anew by his sudden inability to look at her, Malena beckoned him, grabbing the envelopes from his hand when he got close enough.

"Orval is also here, Malena," her manservant said.

She sighed as she rifled through the envelopes. "Have him wait in my sitting room."

Sven nodded, bowed and shuffled backwards out through the door. Malena sunk in the bath, keeping her hands high above the water. She'd lost more than one paper to inattention and these she couldn't afford to lose. The interest to be paid was growing and would soon look insurmountable.

Growling, Malena climbed out of the tub. Her desk would hold the answers she needed to her finances. With the towel loosely wrapped around her, she stomped from the bathing room. She dug out her key and opened her desk, rifling through the neatly arranged papers.

Her accountant had sent a recent list of her assets and she'd been avoiding looking at it. She opened it now, eyes quickly scanning over the figures. It was worse than she'd feared.

"Malena?"

Orval stood with one foot in her bedroom, one foot in her study. He balked at the look on her face.

"I'm sorry," he stuttered. "I thought I heard you in here and… I'll go!" He backed out of the room quickly, shutting the door behind him.

Malena realized she'd been clutching at the papers in her hand, crumpling them. They only told her what she'd already known. It was past time for a new husband. She caught sight of her reflection in the framed picture of her brother she kept on her desk. She looked too old for a husband, even with the newest batch of perfume.

Putting away all the papers, including the notes of promise, Malena wandered out of the study. Orval was perched in her sitting room, hands wringing between his knees. He looked up when she entered, pausing, as he had done, on the threshold.

Malena frowned at him, thinking. This was a pure man, a rarity from what she knew of men. His eyes were wide, looking at her. He trusted her more than he should have.

"Orval," she said, drawing out his name. "You don't have a wife or children, do you?"

He shook his head. "No. Oh, no. I would have told you."

She believed him, oddly enough. "And your parents?"

"Gone," he told her with little emotion. "Gone a while."

"Hmm." His old employer might be the only connection he had. She entered the room more fully, still only wearing a towel. His eyes trailed after her as she paced in front of him. "How old do you think I am, Orval?"

Stopping, she pivoted to face him. It took a moment for his eyes to find her face. She smiled at him. There was a glimmer of confusion in his eyes. He hadn't yet learned not to discuss age with women, further cementing him as an innocent in Malena's eyes.

He squinted at her. "I'm not really sure. Four and twenty?"

Malena flushed. She shouldn't look as old as that. Resisting the impulse to rush to her vanity, she laughed instead, drawing close enough to pat Orval on the cheek.

"Orval, you really are innocent, aren't you?" She should have been delighted with the age he chose. Her reality was much different but instead all she could think of was that no man would want her looking so old.

He didn't answer, staring up at her as though she was his world. It would be all too simple to lure him down into the cellar. Possibly the best perfume she might ever make would come from him. While the leather journal asked for the true innocents, children, not even Malena would stoop to that. She wasn't even sure she would be able to offer Orval.

Rising up from his seat, he wrapped his arms around her, leaning her into him. Surprised, it took her a moment to loosen into his grasp. The towel slipped as her arms went up to surround him.

"Is there anything the matter?" Orval asked into her ear, actually sounding concerned.

Malena sighed. "Nothing new. Just the same worries as always."

"You need a husband, don't you?"

Surprised at his insight, she pulled back to look at him. His eyes were sad and Malena couldn't figure out what to make of it. While she enjoyed his company, perhaps more than she should and more than she'd enjoyed anyone in her recent memory, they'd only known each other a short time.

"You're becoming attached," she scolded him. "I told you not to."

Orval grinned. "I can't help myself. You're making it too easy."

Malena could think of hundreds of things she could tell him to make it too difficult. She wondered what he would make of the cellar. She frowned, thinking of her workroom again.

Brushing the thoughts away, she drew Orval towards the bedroom, leaving her towel behind on the floor. Orval followed her willingly and Malena allowed herself to become lost in him for a time. It drove her worries from her mind, his simplicity and his trust.

But later, when Orval was sleeping, muttering and snoring, Malena climbed from the bed. A square piece of paper sat propped up on her vanity. She crossed the room to inspect it.

The invite promised to her the night before. She wasn't sure when her manservant had delivered it. Perhaps with the notes of promise? Unlike him not to tell her about it though. Sitting at the small bench, she turned the invitation over in her hands.

Her reflection was impossible to ignore and Malena ended up staring at herself. Four and twenty. She needed to look much younger than that to capture a husband, especially the sort she needed to maintain her lifestyle. Dabbing on some more of her perfume, Malena breathed in its scent.

Its effects were almost entirely unnoticeable. The first dab always let her know what she could expect from it. Any use after that was purely maintenance. She was stuck at this age until she found someone else. Orval groaned, flinging an arm out to dangle over the side of the bed.

He was the easy answer. And the hard answer. Every person who'd gone down into her cellar had earned it, in one way or another. She'd been surprised by how ineffective the perfume her attacker of last night had created. He must have been worse than she'd thought. It was all turning out so poorly.

Sighing, Malena stood up again, feeling restless. Wrapping herself in a silk dressing gown, Malena left the room. She found her manservant in the cellar, cleaning up. She wrinkled her nose at the familiar but pungent stenches created by another batch of perfume.

"Malena! You don't need to be down here. I'm cleaning," Sven said, looking mortified to find her down there. "You're looking much better," he tacked on as an afterthought.

"Not good enough though," she groused. "Sven, how is our list in Capeland?"

His eyes widened in the gloom. "I haven't had time to create a list, Malena. And…" He looked around the basement, his expression tinged with confusion. "Do we need a list just yet?"

"Orval says I look four and twenty. Three men refused me at the ball last night. I trust you've seen the notes of promise."

Sven nodded cautiously, his hand tightening around the brush he held.

"I don't know if I can find us a new husband like this."

His eyes scraped over her face. "But I left an invitation on your vanity."

"I know you did. Thank you. But that does not indicate anything. I'm intended for an old man. Those won't do, you know."

"I know," Sven agreed. "I can start a list."

"Will you be able to find what I'm looking for within a week?"

He looked doubtful, making her worry even more. Sven had always managed before. He had a nose for the dissolute men of society that wouldn't be missed. He also knew where she drew the line.

"What about Orval?" Sven asked.

Malena's mouth twisted. "I know. He would be perfect but…"

There was no judgment on Sven's face. He never judged her. He would do anything for her and in turn, she kept him safe and hidden. Asking him for advice was a ridiculous thought. Malena sighed, feeling alone. How she wished she could find the right husband. None of the past ones had been what they needed.

"I'll think on it and when you're done here, perhaps you can go hunting," she told him.

Sven bobbed his head and returned to cleaning. He was a little simple, broken by years of abuse. Malena growled at the guilty voice in her head and returned to her bedroom. Orval still slept, peacefully. She would give Sven the week.

He found nothing, becoming more and more frantic as the dinner came closer and closer. Malena tried to hide her own panic. She wasn't sure how she'd let them come to this. The notes of promise were still flooding in and she had nothing to pay them with. Orval could sense the tension and did his best to dispel it but he was only making it worse.

The night before the dinner, Malena was toying with the invitation. Orval was stretched out on the bed, watching her. When she didn't respond to her name being called, he went to her.

"Another event?" he asked, snatching the invitation from her hands.

"Yes."

"Will this be the one?"

"Hopefully."

"I wish you didn't have to do this."

Malena was starting to wish the same thing. It was dangerous and she watched him in her looking glass. He was frowning over the invitation and she closed her eyes, etching the image onto the backs of her eyelids.

"Have I ever shown you my cellar, Orval?"

Sven fastened the back of her emerald necklace, stroking the shining gems with gentle fingers. Malena smiled at him through the looking glass, reaching up to touch his hand. Startled, he glanced down at her.

"We'll be fine, Sven. I feel good about this dinner."

He smiled at her. Sven never seemed to think about a future where she wouldn't be able to take care of him.

Uncapping her perfume, Malena swiped two strips down her neck. She didn't even bother checking to make sure her appearance was at its best. Either it was, or it wasn't. She'd either done enough or she hadn't.

"You look beautiful, Malena," Sven said in hushed tones.

She stood, her long gown almost bowling over the small bench in front of her vanity.

"Would you like a ride in the carriage?" Malena asked him.

He nodded, reaching out to twine his fingers in hers. Malena grinned and tugged him out of her bedroom and down the stairs. There was something oddly hopeful about the night and the two of them stepped out into the fresh air.

Sven delighted at the bumpy ride over the cobblestone of Capeland's center. He was pressed against the window, almost crouched on the ground, trying to get as close to everything they passed as possible. Malena watched him, trying to ignore the guilt that always seemed to hover around her whenever he was enjoying something in such a child-like manner.

"Can I wait in the carriage for you?" Sven asked.

"Of course. I even brought a blanket, in case you wanted to." He would fall asleep waiting for her.

"No one will find us," Sven whispered to the glass. "Never find us."

Malena looked away. She tried to recapture some of the hopefulness and cheer she'd felt earlier. Her fingers twirled the invitation around and around.

"I love you," Sven said, startling Malena.

"I love you too," she replied. "And I'm going to fix everything tonight."

Sven started singing as they rode. It was a cavalry song that she'd heard their father whistle over and over.

"Into battle, Malena," Sven said as the carriage stopped.

She grinned at him and saluted, stepping out of the door as it was opened for her.

Malena was seated next to Malcom's uncle, as she'd expected. And also as she'd expected, he was much older than any man she'd ever married, let alone considered marrying. He didn't leer at her as she sat, surprising her.

"You are aware that Malcom has purposely placed us next to one another," he leaned over to say after introductions were made.

She smiled at him warmly. Reaching over to lightly touch his arm, she said, "I know."

Once the dinner began, Malena split her attention. Robinard, Malcom's uncle, had two sons. She was hoping one of them would be more likely. In all reality, it would be a struggle for either of them to be less likely than their father. One was perhaps a bit too young and probably lacking the funds she needed. He still appeared to be a better option than Robinard.

But Malena did not betray her thoughts to her dinner companion. Malena flirted with Robinard, carefully prying out pertinent tidbits. He'd been widowed eight years and was only now interested in finding a new wife. He surprised her consistently with his virtuousness and guilelessness. There was no cattiness in his conversation.

"I worry about my eldest," he told her, delving into personal conversation. Malena turned to hear more. "I hope that a good woman might settle him down as Eva did for me."

His gaze swung to his oldest child and Malena's followed. The young man in question was laughing uproariously at something Malcom had leaned over to whisper in his ear.

"Malcom isn't the best of influences," Robinard said with a frown. Then he straightened, turning to stare at her. "I didn't intend to burden you with the complexities of child-rearing."

Malena looked at him. Then she looked at his son. If she wanted the son, she had the feeling that Robinard would approve despite clearly liking her himself.

"-oddly comfortable," Robinard said.

Malena missed the start of the sentence. Shifting in her seat, she smiled at him neutrally. The woman on his other side asked him a question, freeing Malena from the momentary awkwardness. Her mind was winding its way through her options and the differences among them.

Looking out of the window situated on the other side, she focused on the glow of the lamp on the street. The dining room was at the front of the house, providing her with an easy view of the sidewalk. It was an uninspiring view but Malena still had the sudden urge to be out there, instead of tucked inside the echoing dining room with strangers.

She shook her head, scolding herself. Out of the corner of her eye, she saw a blur of color that didn't belong outside in the darkness. The other window didn't hold a street lamp but somewhere, such a thing illuminated a familiar figure.

Orval was watching her through the window. His face wasn't entirely clear but Malena knew who it was. He lifted a hand and Malena let her fingers rise in a small salute. A grin broke out over his face. She stared at him, wondering when he'd had a chance to look at the address on her invitation. While she was wondering, he disappeared.

"-to your liking?" Robinard asked her.

Flustered, Malena turned back to her host. She blinked at him in confusion while he glanced at her in concern.

"Is everything to your liking?" he repeated.

Malena looked down at her plate. She hadn't even noticed the next course. It was a rare cut of sirloin. Blood seeped out onto the plate. Reaching up to stroke her mostly-empty perfume bottle, Malena looked away from the plate, up at Robinard.

"It's a bit bloody for me," she told him with a small grimace. Her stomach turned over under the constricting satin of her dress.

He nodded understandingly. "It's not to everyone's taste, I know. You'll enjoy the next course though," he told her, going on to detail it for her.

Malena nodded along, only half listening. Instead, she was watching her host. He genuinely seemed to care about her tastes and had waved someone over to fetch her plate away. Maybe she didn't need a younger husband that she would eventually have to dispose of.

Robinard was wealthy, kind and old enough that she would be assured a life after his was done. He didn't seemed concerned that she wasn't young like the women competing for his sons' attention. He didn't appear to notice that in the least.

Perhaps she wouldn't have to maintain herself and Sven through artificial and bloody means. Already she'd broken her pattern by letting Orval leave the cellar as whole as he'd gone in. Perhaps there were other patterns that wouldn't suffer from the breaking.

"It's refreshing to meet someone who has also lost a spouse," Robinard said as he speared a pear on the end of his fork.

Malena nodded, still watching him for signs that there was a monster underneath the fine façade. She'd seen no glint of one as of yet and she fancied herself a keen observer of humanity.

"Though it is probably for the best that you have no children. I find mine more than enough," he laughed. His eyes glimmered at her in the candlelight, the wrinkles around his eyes smiling.

If there was a monster hiding, Malena could handle that. She'd handled plenty of monsters in her lifetime. Maybe this one time, she would find a gentleman instead.

AFTERWORD

Thanks for reading!

ALSO BY THE AUTHOR:

NOVELS
Born in the Mouth of an Angel
Born on the Run
Born from the Ashes
Born for a Better Life

THE SWAMP CHILDREN
Novels
A Swamp of Bones
A Swamp of Souls
A Swamp of Lies
Novella
Things in the Swamp
Short Stories
The Swamp Witches

NOVELLAS
The Locket
The Amaranthine Dowager
The Poisoned Perfume

SHORT STORIES

Just Another Shop
Just Another Customer
The Problem of Carl and Louie
Patience, Violence and the Red, Red Moon
The Twisted Tree
Tricks, Games & Insanity
Leipreachán
The Gothic Ghost Killer

ABOUT THE AUTHOR

Abigail Fero is an American fantasy writer whose work is bound by a love of the unreal and the impossible. She hopes that you'll find something to enjoy in her body of work. You can find her books online and find out more about her on her website: abigailfero.blogspot.com

www.ingramcontent.com/pod-product-compliance
Lightning Source LLC
Chambersburg PA
CBHW071233170626
46809CB00008BA/3027